Crave

ADDICTED TO YOU #1

K. M. SCOTT

Books by K.M. Scott

If I Dream (Corrupted Love #1)
If You Fight (Corrupted Love #2)
If We Fall (Corrupted Love #3)

Crash Into Me (Heart of Stone #1)
Fall Into Me (Heart of Stone #2)
Give In To Me (Heart of Stone #3)
Heart of Stone Volume One Box Set
Ever After (Heart of Stone #4)
A Heart of Stone Christmas (Heart of Stone #5)
Unforgettable (Heart of Stone #6)
Unbreakable (Heart of Stone #7)
Heart of Stone Volume Two Box Set

Temptation (Club X #1)
Surrender (Club X #2)
Possession (Club X #3)
Satisfaction (Club X #4)
Acceptance (Club X #5)

Crave (Addicted To You #1)
Adore (Addicted To You #2)
Shatter (Addicted To You #3)
Claim (Addicted To You #4)

Books by K.M. Scott writing as Gabrielle Bisset

Blood Avenged (Sons of Navarus #1)

Blood Betrayed (Sons of Navarus #2)

Longing (A Sons of Navarus Short Story)

Blood Spirit (Sons of Navarus #3)

The Deepest Cut (A Sons of Navarus Short Story)

Blood Prophecy (Sons of Navarus #4)

Blood Craving (Sons of Navarus #5)

Blood Eclipse (Sons of Navarus #6)

The Sons of Navarus Box Set #1

The Sons of Navarus Box Set #2

Stolen Destiny (Destined Ones Duology #1)

Destiny Redeemed (Destined Ones Duology #2)

Love's Master

Masquerade

The Victorian Erotic Romance Trilogy

I want her. I crave her. She's my addiction.
The world knows me as Ian Anwell, New York
Times bestselling author, but Kristina makes
me want more.
Much more.

I need him. I love him. He's my obsession.
Everyone thinks they know Kristina Richards,
but I'm more than what they see on the screen.
So much more.

I'm his muse, and this is our story.

Crave was previously published as SILK Volume
One.

CHAPTER ONE

Ian

A WARM PUFF of air against my cheek rouses me from my sleep, reminding me that no matter how sunny it seemed as I looked out my window a few hours ago, fall has arrived with a vengeance. I roll over onto my back and stare up at the ceiling as the forced heat now blows over my head. The floor in my living room pushes hard against my back tonight. I should be used to the feeling, but I'm not and I wince from the pain shooting up from the base of my spine.

To my left on the floor next to me stands a half-empty bottle of twelve-year-old scotch, my companion tonight. Standing guard even as I dropped off, it waits for me to remember how much I love its contents.

Grabbing the neck, I cradle the bottle to my chest as I contemplate getting up and away from the air heating my head. I own a five million dollar apartment in New York City, and I spend my nights getting blasted and ending up on the floor. My neighbors would never imagine that's who I am. New York Times bestselling author Ian Anwell, author of historical fiction bestsellers Caligula's Dream and Nero's Nightmare and favorite of readers worldwide, a fall down drunk and forever recovering heroin addict.

My publisher keeps the whole addict thing carefully under wraps. Completely hush-hush. All I have to do is keep clean and continue writing one book a year for them, and they'll keep paying me the ridiculously large advances I've grown accustomed to. The problem is that keeping clean means something must replace the smack, so that's where alcohol comes in and why it's my nearly constant companion.

But I've grown tired of waking up on the floor in a drunken haze lately and the itch to go back to my old ways gets stronger and stronger every day. I'm an addict before I'm anything else, and I need a new fix.

My phone rings, so I make my way to the couch to answer it. Swiping the screen, I see it's my agent, Sheila Rogers. A likable woman, if not appealing, she seems to have been able to overcome what nature or God, depending on your beliefs, forced on her looks-wise to become a successful literary agent. Absurdly tall for a female, she reaches nearly my six foot two inch height, and on some days when she does her hair in this upswept thing she likes for formal affairs, she towers over me like some Amazon woman.

I've known tall women, but they've all been models. Poor Sheila could never be mistaken for a model, though.

Not that I give a fuck about what she looks like. I don't want to fuck her. I just need her to keep doing the bang up job selling my books she's always done for me. But I do wonder sometimes how a woman who looks like she does got past her appearance to get where she is today. An almost grotesquely tall woman with gangly limbs and a plain face isn't exactly what anyone imagines when they think of a successful woman, but she's achieved what others haven't and I'd be lost without her, at least professionally.

I answer the call and her one true blessing comes through loud and clear. Sheila's voice is what I imagine an angel's voice would sound like. Not too soft, not too rough, and smooth as silk, it's what's usually called a radio voice.

"Hi, Sheila," I croak out before I clear my throat.

"Ian, please tell me I didn't wake you up. It's not even eight o'clock on a Tuesday night. Are you okay?"

I want to say something about okay being relative, but that will only make her nervous and she'll call again every night until she's convinced I'm not filling my body full of shit again.

So I lie.

"I'm fine, Sheila. What are you doing working so late?"

"I have good news. I think we're close to selling the film rights to Caligula's Dream. I've gotten the deal to be as sweet as I think it can be, but you're going to like it. They have big plans for the film, and as you demanded, they're willing to let you be an executive producer and the main writer on the project."

"This is good news. I knew you'd get them to come around. You always do. You're my secret weapon, Sheila," I say, my words slurring slightly.

In all honesty, she's my only weapon since the agent I used to have for film deals dumped me after my last stint in rehab. Sheila stepped in to help without one complaint, like the savior she is.

"Ian, you sound wrong. Are you really okay?" she asks in her angelic voice I hate lying to.

"I'm fine. Well, maybe I'm coming down with something. You know how it is when the seasons change. I think I'm going to hang out on the couch and nurse myself through whatever this is."

"Please promise me you're not planning on doing anything to derail your career, which I've so assiduously worked to make the stunning success that it is."

"I promise. Don't worry, Sheila."

She remains silent for a long moment, as if she's assessing the truthfulness of my words, and then finally changing the subject, she asks, "Have you gotten any ideas for your next book? They've already asked a few times."

They is my publisher, and I knew they would be. Nero's Nightmare soared up the charts, hitting the number one spot on the Times list the first week it was out. They'd be fools not to want to continue our relationship. But I don't have any ideas for the next book, even though they think asking me repeatedly will make the ideas come faster.

"I know, but you can't rush this kind of thing."

The truth is I haven't even tried to work in weeks. I simply have no ideas for what to do next.

"I understand, and you know how I appreciate the artistic temperament. I'll tell them you're working on ideas and put them off for a few weeks more. Just tell me you're going to work on it, Ian."

"I'm going to work on it," I lie.

Other than drinking, I have no plans to do anything except watch movies alone in my apartment, unless I can count craving the worst thing in the world as work.

"Okay. I'll check on you next week. You know you can call me whenever you need to, right?" she asks, omitting the other words she wants to say. I hear in her voice her fear that I'm about to turn back to the life she's had to rescue me from far too many times before.

"I know, and thank you, Sheila. Have a good night."

"You too, Ian. And congratulations again on Nero's Nightmare. You deserve it. That book's the best one yet."

"Thanks, Sheila. Goodbye."

I toss the phone on the couch next to me and lean back to close my eyes. She's right. Nero's Nightmare is my best work yet, but I want something different. My brain craves something new, something challenging. I'm sure I could find that if my brain could just let go and allow the ideas to come, but the scotch isn't doing the job.

A sharp craving stabs at me, and for a moment all my brain can think of is how to score. I have to fight the desire, but it's like second nature and my body wants it. My limbs ache as the phantom feeling of getting high flows through my mind.

Just a little is all it would take.

Grabbing the remote, I turn on the TV and hope I can find something to take my mind off what I want more than anything at the moment. Clicking through channels, I see nothing to distract me. A thousand channels and nothing but shit.

Then I see her.

Long brown hair the color of cocoa, the truest brown I've ever seen. That's the first thing I notice about her. The camera moves in and I see her eyes, blue like the flowers on my mother's Corningware casserole dishes she had handed down to her from my grandmother. My eyes travel down to the woman's mouth with its full, deep pink lips, and I watch them as she speaks, not giving a damn about the words leaving her mouth but intensely focused on how it moves so seductively, like every word she utters is sexual and alluring.

Who is she?

I press the Info button on the remote and quickly scan the details about the film, my gaze coming to rest on her name.

Kristina Richards.

Kristina. I say her name, loving the feel of my tongue as it caresses the back of my teeth to form the second and third syllables. Kristina. I repeat it over and over until she's all I can think of.

The camera pans back and for the first time I can see her completely. She's thin but not sickly looking like so many skinny Hollywood actresses whose faces look beautiful but when you look below their necks their bodies are all sharp edges and boniness. She's standing next to some man who at the moment I want to kill I'm so jealous.

I watch the rest of the movie, unable to focus on anything but Kristina. When it's finished, I go back to where I began and watch it all over again. And again. And again five more times. Yet I have no idea what the film is about and I don't care.

All I care about is her.

At two a.m., I realize that I haven't touched a drop of scotch in hours. I pour myself a glass and set it on the coffee table in front of me as I return to studying Kristina Richards. I feel the obsession beginning and let it take me over, feeling it course through me. I've always loved the moment when what I'm addicted to begins to become part of me. The moment it becomes necessary to who I am. History. Writing. Heroin. Alcohol. The rare girlfriend or two I can truly say I cared for.

And now Kristina.

I wonder how it's possible I've never seen her before. As someone who spends the majority of his days in his home, I watch more television and movies than anyone else I've ever heard of, and yet she's eluded me until now.

The film I've found her in—a remake of The Misfits, I think—might be good. Not that I care. She's all I'm interested in. After I've watched it eight times, I need more, and with just a few clicks of my remote, I can watch every film she's ever made.

Netflix is like an addict's worst nightmare or best friend. I guess it depends on how you see people like me. I scroll through the choices and decide to start at the top. By the time the city below begins to come alive for another workday, I realize that I've seen some of these films but never saw her.

That's how it is with addictions and obsessions. One day something means nothing to you, and then the next day it's all you can think about.

By the third day, I need more. I've watched all her movies, but that's not enough. I want to see her in person. Thankfully, my success comes with certain perks that have nothing to do with being able to afford expensive things.

I can get things other people can't.

A quick call to my publicist will do the trick. Albert is night to Sheila's day. Where she's sweet and I think genuinely worries about me, he seems to be rushed and disinterested nearly all the time. His lack of appreciation for what I do irritates me too, but in this case, I'll tolerate him if he can help me get what I want.

"Ian Anwell, how the hell are you?" Albert asks in his hurried way that tells me this is a rhetorical question. All the better. I'm not interested in talking about how I feel.

"Albert, I want you to set up a meeting with Kristina Richards."

"Who?"

"Kristina Richards, the actress. I want to meet her, so do your magic and make it happen."

He's silent for a minute and then says, "Okay. What should I tell her manager you want?"

The thought of what I want from her races through my mind, making my cock stiffen, and I lick my lips in anticipation. "Tell her I'm a fan. Tell her I'm interested in speaking to her to research my next book. For fuck's sake, Albert. I'm a New York Times bestselling author of four books."

"Actresses don't usually read much historical fiction, Ian."

Albert's place in my world seems to be to keep me humble. He's doing a hell of a job too. "Fine. Tell her I'm a huge fan."

"Okay, I'll see what I can do. I'll let you know

what I find out."

I throw the phone away from me, disgusted by my publicist's humility refresher. I would have asked Sheila to do it, but that caring for me thing she does is a double-edged sword. She can't seem to keep good news to herself. At least Albert can, which is why I always ask him to do things like this.

Like when I needed to speak to a world-renowned expert on Roman sex practices and couldn't get past the man's officious secretary. I never did figure out why she took such a disliking to me from just one phone call, but she wasn't going to let me get to speak to him come hell or high water. Just one call from Albert, however, coupled with a bouquet of flowers and suddenly she couldn't have been more accommodating.

Things like that are the reason I don't fire Albert and look past how little I like him. But if he doesn't succeed with Kristina's manager, I might have to consider finding a new publicist.

I return to watching her movies, preferring not to research anything about her online. That might seem somewhat ironic considering what I do for a living, but as much as I love the idea of stalking someone on the Internet, I find it unfulfilling in practice. So what if I can learn every little thing about a person courtesy of nosy websites and hacks masquerading as journalists? That kind of research lacks vigor, lacks flesh and blood.

If I could learn about ancient cultures by living among them, I would. Instead, I'm forced to research in books and secondhand sources. Finding out about someone living now shouldn't be relegated to stalking from afar, hidden behind the anonymity of the Internet. That's the coward's way.

No, I want to meet Kristina in person. I want to look into those blue eyes. I want to listen to her soft voice as she sits just inches away from me. I want to smell her perfume and the scent her shampoo leaves in her hair. I want to feel the softness of her skin on mine. I want to taste her and savor the delicate flavor of her body on the tip of my tongue as I tease her just before I bury my face in her pussy.

I fantasize about how incredible it will be when I slide my cock into her until my phone ringing disturbs me from my daydreaming. Looking down at the screen, I see it's Albert.

"Ian, I was wrong about actresses not reading your stuff. Seems you have a fan. She'll be at Jax's at seven tonight. I figured somewhere hidden away would be best. Her manager said she knew exactly what you look like. Thank God I convinced you to change that terrible light grey suit to the black one for your book jacket picture."

"Yeah, thanks Albert. Good call."

"Good luck, Ian."

Albert's good news spurs my creative juices, and I hurry over to my laptop to seize the moment before it leaves me. Sitting down, I begin to tap out whatever pops into my head, and in just minutes I sit amazed at the words on the screen in front of me. Instead of brainstorming for my next historical novel, I've written out the bones of the first scene of something far more erotic.

I let the words flow from my fingers, not caring that I don't usually write in this genre or that I can't imagine how Sheila would react if she found this in her inbox. I lose myself in the story of a woman who uses sex to keep her from her heroin addiction. It's smut, pure and simple, and I can't believe how much I like it.

By six, I've written four pages of my fantasy but it's time to get ready to meet Kristina. After a quick shower, I stand in front of the bathroom mirror checking out my look and questioning whether this meeting was a bad idea. My dark hair hangs in my eyes, and even when I push it back off my face, it still doesn't look right. I give myself a good, close shave, but the face that stares back at me still isn't convinced.

She's a movie star, Ian. If this is all you're bringing, it's not much.

Pointing at the mirror, I push back against that little voice inside my head. "Shut the fuck up. Don't start that shit."

So it whispers back a dark secret that never leaves me. *You'd be much better if you had just a little before you went.*

I will myself to forget that evil voice. I promised Sheila. I promised myself. I don't want to get back into that again. I'm clean and I want to stay that way.

My eyes tell the truth I don't want to admit. In their darkness, I see the voice is right. I would be much better if I could get my hands on some to take the edge off. Kristina won't like this Ian—this person who drinks too much to stop himself from doing something much worse and can't even look at himself in the mirror without hating what he sees.

I turn away from that truth, no matter how seductive it is to believe it. It's almost time to go meet Kristina. I can do this without help.

CHAPTER TWO

Ian

J AX'S IS AN out-of-the-way bar on the West side and a favorite of mine because there's not a booth in the place that isn't dark and secluded. That's how a bar should be. Unless you're some frat boy, getting blasted in public should be private affair. I walk in and nod at the bartender, a tall, thin man who looks to be in his late forties, if his slightly greying hair is any indication. The lighter color peppers near his temples and the top of his head giving him a look that reminds me of the serious cop on every TV police drama, and as I pass, he gives me the guy chin lift acknowledgement.

I scan the bar for any sign of Kristina and see her sitting with her head down at a booth all the way in the back. As I slowly make my way there, I notice how small she seems there surrounded by the high-backed wooden booth. Her brown hair is lighter than in her movies, but I like it this honeyed caramel color.

"Hi, Kristina," I say in a low voice.

She looks up and I see those gorgeous cornflower blue eyes. Even better in person, they sparkle with interest as she studies me for a quick moment before she says quietly, "It's nice to meet you, Ian. You look just like your picture on your books."

Her smile is far shyer than I expect from a Hollywood starlet, charming me more than I thought she could just seconds into our meeting. I sit down and stare across the table at this beautiful woman who I'm surprised even knows who I am. A thousands things come to me, but I say none of them, sure they're all wrong for this moment.

Instead, I smile and extend my hand to shake hers. "Hi, Kristina. Thanks for agreeing to meet me. It's an honor."

Her hand gently grips mine as she blushes from my compliment, but all I can think of is how excited my body immediately becomes from her touch. She says something about it being a bigger honor to meet a New York Times bestselling author, but I'm focused on the fantasy that's forming in my mind about her hand and how it would feel wrapped around my cock as she slides all of me into her mouth.

She takes her hand away and smiles shyly

again, layering charm on top of my desire for her. "I was so excited to hear from my manager that you wanted to meet me. I've read all your books. I love history and your books make it even more interesting. You have a way of making your characters come alive right on the pages."

"Thank you. I guess we're both fans because I've seen every one of your films and love them. Every one of them."

Kristina blushes again. "That's so nice of you to say. I try to improve with each project. I've been very fortunate to be offered roles that allow me to stretch my abilities."

She continues to talk about her career, and to be honest, I find myself becoming more enchanted by the moment. Behind the beautiful exterior exists a serious actor. I hadn't expected that, and as she explains how she's hoping to snag a role in some film that begins to shoot in Canada in a few weeks, I'm genuinely interested in what she has to say.

It doesn't take long for our meeting to go a way I hadn't planned. I'd wanted to meet her and hopefully get her back to my place to fuck her, but as I listen to her speak about her films and my books, that idea is eclipsed by another.

I want her to be my muse. With every word that comes out of that gorgeous mouth, I'm more convinced that she's my muse for Silk, the erotica book I'm writing. I can't tell her that now, though, since I just met her. I don't want to scare her off.

"Listen to me rambling on about myself and my movies all this time. I'm sorry."

Her beautiful eyes fill with regret, but I shake my head, hoping to dispel any shame she feels. "It's wonderful to listen to someone so dedicated to their craft. Please don't feel like you should stop. I'm all ears."

"Tell me about you. I know what the blurb at the end of your books says, but I bet you're even more interesting than that. How do you come up with ideas for your books? It must be so difficult."

I admit something I never tell anyone, oddly comfortable enough already with her to share my secret. "It is. The pressure to create a story that not only stands up to the last one but surpasses it can make finding ideas very difficult."

Her eyes light up with a look of recognition. "You're like that too? I always try to do better than I did before, but it does put a lot of pressure on me. We're probably our own worst critics, you know that?"

A pretty waitress with her blond hair pulled tightly up into a bun interrupts us for our drink order and since the place is practically empty, she returns quickly with Kristina's white wine and my scotch. I know I shouldn't get drunk and even though this is going pretty well, I sense the demons inside whispering that I'm boring her and I could have been so much more interesting if I just snorted a little before I came here.

Kristina slips off her white sweater to reveal a pale pink long sleeve shirt that hugs her body in all the right places. The camera may add ten pounds, but she appears slightly heavier in person. Not heavy like fat but healthy looking, like a woman should be.

"Do you get to read a lot?" I ask, wondering if she might be willing to become my muse.

She shakes her head and frowns, like she's disappointed at the answer she's about to give. "No. My work schedule makes it difficult, but I always fit your books in."

"You don't have to say that. I know your life is probably far more exciting than reading my historical fiction."

I'm not usually so humble and self-effacing, but Kristina has charmed me into being something nicer than my usual self.

"Oh no. I always read your books as soon as they come out. I've been a fan since I read Caligula's Dream."

The idea that the gorgeous woman in front of

me read my book on corruption in the reign of Caligula thrills me, oddly enough. I've been at signings where hundreds of people have waited in line for hours to talk to me as I scribble my name on the title page of their books and never felt as incredible as I do at the moment when she says that.

Raising my glass, I offer a toast to the two of us. "To fulfilling careers and meeting others who appreciate our work."

Kristina gently clinks her glass against mine. "And to finding new people who understand you."

I hear a sense of loneliness in her voice despite the smile she wears. A mouthful of scotch slides down my throat, warming my insides as it makes me feel braver by the second. I want to touch her left hand as it rests on the table. To reach over and run my fingertip over the knuckles and feel her soft skin against mine again.

"If only I'd thought to bring my book with me, then I could ask you to sign it," she says with sadness, her frown deeper now. "I can't believe I ran out of my apartment without remembering it."

"I can walk you back to your place and sign it there, if you like," I offer, hoping she'll take me up on it.

Her eyes light up again. "That would be great! You wouldn't mind?"

"It would be my pleasure."

"I don't have scotch at my place, though. All I have is wine. Is that okay?"

"I'm fine," I lie, as if drinking isn't an integral part of what keeps me together and off something much worse.

Kristina slips back into her sweater, ready to go. "Okay, then let's head there now! My place isn't too far."

I mentally file away the information that we both live in the same neighborhood and follow her out toward the street. As I walk behind her through the bar, my gaze fixes on her ass in a black skirt that falls to just above her knees and shows off her shapely lower body. Not generally a man who finds asses much to care about, I can't take my eyes off hers. Not too big and not too small, it fills out the skirt like the fabric knows exactly where to cling to make anyone behind her want to cup their hand over that ass.

We hit the bracing October air and it's like a hard slap to the face. Kristina seems unmoved by the chilliness, though, and takes my hand in hers. "It's just a few blocks so we can walk. Unless you want to take a cab? You look a little cold."

"I'm good. What kind of New Yorker would I

be if I couldn't handle the little chill in the fall air that accompanies the turning of the leaves and that earthy autumn smell?"

She beams at me and tugs me toward her place. "I love the way you say things, Ian. Every word sounds so perfect."

If only she knew how imperfect and downright damaged the man she clung to at that moment was she might not be so enthralled by my choice of words.

We walk together as we talk about the weather, living in the city, and how she's going to hate being away if she has to leave to film in Vancouver, and all the while I feel my demons one by one retreat to their hiding places deep inside me until all that's left of me wants what she offers.

Sweetness.

Lightness.

Happiness.

But I don't know those anymore, so they're strangers to me. What I know is that the obsession that began as I watched her on my TV screen is morphing into something far more serious that I won't be able to fight.

Or won't want to fight.

I feel a tug on my arm and Kristina says, "Here we are! Up two flights and there I am."

Her building is a brownstone typical of many New York neighborhoods. I let her lead me up the front stairs and then up two flights of stairs, listening to her talk about how she found this place before she hit it big and still loves it, even though everyone says she should move to a more upscale apartment. I sense she's nervous all of a sudden, if the speed of the words tumbling out of her mouth now is any indication.

Her apartment certainly isn't what a Hollywood star would usually have, but it's cozy. One bedroom, a kitchen, and a living room that looks out onto the street, it's got a charm that most small apartments in New York City don't possess. Decorated in no particular style, the walls have pictures of Kristina and her co-stars from some of her films hung beside inexpensive artwork of vases with flowers.

She offers me a seat on her couch, a leather piece that looks odd among much cheaper furnishings around it, and I sit down while she finds her copy of my book on her bookshelf. She hasn't lied. A floor to ceiling bookshelf covers one wall with all her books, and as I scan the titles, I'm impressed. Kristina reads many of my contemporaries in the historical fiction genre, a fact that surprises me, but I'm particularly impressed by three Colleen McCullough Masters of Rome books near mine.

"I'm situated amongst some greats there," I say as she pulls Caligula's Dream off a middle shelf.

"A few of these were my mother's. She always loved history, and I guess I take after her."

"Did you enjoy McCullough's Antony and Cleopatra?"

She sits next to me and holds my book out for me to take along with a pen. "I did. She has a wonderful way of making that time period come to life like you do. Thank you so much for this."

I sign my name and a few words about her being my biggest fan, but all I can think of is how her knee feels nudging against my thigh as she sits next to me with her legs folded underneath her. When I hand her the book, she smiles so sweetly at my inscription.

"Thank you. It's perfect."

More perfection from the world's most imperfect soul. If she only knew.

Kristina shifts her weight and begins to fidget with her hands. "I guess you know all about that whole thing with John Stinson and think I'm just the biggest fool, don't you?"

I truly have no idea what she's referring to, but I can see by the pain in her gorgeous eyes that it's something she's embarrassed by. With a smile,

I say, "I don't know what you mean."

"You don't?"

Shaking my head, I explain I rarely watch anything that would tell me about Hollywood gossip. "So you see, I really don't know what you mean."

"Oh. I thought maybe that was why you didn't make a move when we got back here."

She presses her lips together as she waits for my answer, but I'm not in the mood to explain why I haven't tried to kiss her yet. Better to just do it. Sometimes words get in the way.

The fantasy that's been playing on a constant loop in my brain is about to come true. Taking her chin between my thumb and forefinger, I gently pull her face toward me to kiss that delicious mouth I first noticed days ago, dying to know what her perfectly formed lips will feel like as I press mine to them.

My cock is rock hard already, and I haven't even touched her yet. Normally, it takes at least some decent foreplay to get me going, but that's probably because of the poison flowing through me. Now my bulge is practically busting out of my pants before we even kiss.

Just before her mouth meets mine, she moans ever so slightly a tiny whimper, and then we kiss. Her lips are soft and full, and all I can think of as her tongue slides tentatively into my mouth is how much I want to feel those lips and tongue on my cock.

Her hands caress my cheeks as our kiss intensifies, and then she's on my lap straddling my hips, her black skirt up around her waist. My hands instinctively move to cup that beautiful ass I'd admired as we left the bar, and a jolt of excitement courses through me when I feel skin instead of the cotton or silk of panties. Fuck, she's wearing only a garter belt under her skirt!

That gorgeous, full ass feels incredible in my hands. My fingers knead her silky skin as she grinds against the front of my pants, and I lift my hips off the couch to push my cock against her.

Our kiss deepens and our tongues dance together. Kristina moans into my mouth, and I squeeze her cheeks hard, loving how eager she is. She tugs on my hair, her desire ratcheting up against mine and I slip a finger down toward her drenched pussy.

I want her. I want to live the fantasy that's played repeatedly in my mind since that first moment her beautiful face filled my eyes.

Kristina's fingers slide down over my neck to my shirt, and she begins to unbutton it, whispering against my lips, "I want you, Ian. That's why when my manager told me you wanted to meet me, I made the meeting for as soon as possible. Tell me you want me. Tell me what you want me to do."

I push her hands away and groan, "Take your sweater off."

She obeys my command and slips it off, revealing a pink lace bra. I want to see the gorgeous tits under it, so I quickly unhook it and throw it off to the side as I fill my eyes with the sight of her breasts. Full and firm, they look real, which thrills me even more than I imagined. I cup them in my hands and take one full, deep pink nipple in my mouth, sucking gently at first.

Looking up, I see her watching me, biting her lower lip and whimpering, "Yes…harder…"

Her wish is my command, and I suck her pebbled skin harder into my mouth. I close my eyes and listen to her moans as I bite down gently on her excited nipple. Fuck, she's responsive! I hadn't expected that.

Kristina rolls her hips and begins to rub up against me in earnest. I love the idea that my mouth on her is going to get her off even before I whip my cock out. I feel her juices dampen the front of my pants and look up to see her face show the ecstasy building inside her. Releasing her nipple, I move my head to the other one and take it into my mouth, sucking hard as she pulls my hair.

Her hand slides between us and she fingers her wet pussy, but it gets in my way, so I pull her hand away. Disappointed, she frowns and admits quietly, "That's the only way I can get off."

I say nothing but shake my head, determined now to make her come from anything but her fingers touching her clit. Holding her hands behind her back, I slide my cock out of my pants and stroke it from base to head. I position it at her entrance and look up at her. "Not with me."

She smiles and rolls her hips, taking just the tip of my cock inside her. She's wet but tight. Lowering her mouth to mine, she kisses me long and deep and then slides onto me until I'm balls deep into her hot cunt. Releasing her hands, I grip her hips and won't let her move, loving the feel of being inside her. A rush unlike anything I've ever experienced before courses through me just as she breaks our kiss and whispers in my ear, "Fuck me. Make me come, Ian."

My brain shifts to pure pleasure, and every part of my body has a single goal. Make her come from me fucking her. I release my iron grip on her sides and begin guiding her up and down on my cock, loving the sight of her riding me. She's wild and uninhibited in her pursuit of the orgasm she craves. I want to give that to her as much as I want to come too.

Kristina rocks her hips back and forth, urging my cock to rub up against her G-spot. So open, so responsive, she seduces me and for one of the few times in life, I want another to feel pleasure as much as I feel. Her teeth sink into my shoulder as the first moments of her orgasm overtake her. The gentle squeeze of her cunt around my cock tells me I've given her what no one else has ever been able to give her.

I pull her hair roughly to force her to face me. "Don't look away. I want to see your face when you come."

Those blue eyes soften as her body gives in to mine, and then they close as she comes hard on my cock. I'm so close and the tender squeeze of her inner walls milking me sends me over the edge. I flood her cunt sending jets of cum inside her. The feeling is better than anything else I've ever experienced, even my other addictions.

And she is already an addiction. I know that.

"Oh my God," she moans softly as she collapses against my chest. "I've never been able to get off like that."

There's nothing a man loves to hear more than a woman tell him his cock was able to give her something no other man's cock ever could. It's something primal and animalistic, but it makes him feel like that woman is his.

I know no matter what twists and turns our time together might take, Kristina is mine now. But that has to remain our secret.

Smoothing her damp hair from her forehead, I look deep into her eyes and say, "I need you to promise me whatever we are together is kept private. Will you promise me that, Kristina?"

Her mouth turns down and a pained look crosses her face. "Why?"

I place a tiny kiss on the tip of her nose and shake my head. "Because of who we are. The rest of the world knowing would ruin this. Tabloids, paparazzi, gossip columns in the papers, all that would taint what we are. So I want to keep this like a delicious secret just between the two of us. Will you?"

"Are you ashamed of what we did?"

"No. I just don't want the rest of the world ruining this."

She wants to feel what I gave her again, and I want her more than anything else. She's already my muse, even though I haven't told her. I would when the time was right, which makes keeping us a secret all the more important.

Nodding her head, she whispers against my lips, "I promise."

I kiss her and there as we sit with my cock still

deep inside her, I think about how I want to taste that beautiful pussy on the tip of my tongue. Addiction is like that. Once is never enough.

CHAPTER THREE

Kristina

THE AUTUMN SUN streaming in through my bedroom window wakes me, and I stretch my limbs that still ache from the night before. Everything I did with Ian comes flooding back into my mind, and I'm ashamed that I've made the same mistake with another man. I always promise myself that I won't fall so quickly for them, but then I always do.

And then it always ends the same. They leave when I'm already too far gone in love with them and I'm devastated.

I cover my eyes with my arm and wish the regret away as the tears begin to fill my eyes. I can't handle my heart breaking again, but I already know even after just one night together that I'm lost. If only he hadn't been able to get me off like he did.

No, that's not it. I was lost the moment he walked into that bar. So different from any of the usual men I date, he had a look that screamed sensuality as he approached me. Like he enjoyed life more than anyone I'd ever met before. His dark hair that refused to obey his command to stay off his forehead made him look tousled and casual, but his nearly black eyes made him look intense. The combination intrigued me.

Then he spoke and I knew he wasn't like anyone else I'd ever met. Every word that came out of his mouth seemed perfect, like he had a command of language I've never been able to call my own. When I speak, words seem to have a mind of their own and run out of my mouth before I can stop them, but his are so measured and carefully chosen, as if every one of them means the world to him.

I know this is infatuation. I realize that. But it doesn't change that I want to see him again, wishing even as I lie here that he could be next to me right now.

I fall hard and fast for every man, but for the first time, I feel like falling might not be a mistake with Ian. Usually, my boyfriends use me to help their careers by announcing our relationship to the media the day after our first date. Not that I'm not already into them, but it doesn't take long to find out that while I was falling, they were figuring out how being with me would catapult them to the next level and the next movie deal.

But Ian wants to keep what we are a secret. At first I thought he was ashamed of what we'd done, but I don't think so now.

I stretch again, this time feeling an ache in my lower abdomen I've never experienced before. It's a mixture of pain and need, like my body misses him. I look on my phone to check the time and see he's sent me a text. Suddenly I worry he's reconsidered and doesn't want to see me again, preferring to tell me this way instead of having to deal with me in person.

Fear fills me, but I click on the text and read the message he's sent, relief washing over me as I see his perfect words.

I want to be inside you right now, my cock stretching your tight cunt. Until next time, I'll just have to be happy with my memories. Ian

I read his words again and again as my pussy gets wet. I know I shouldn't reply, that I should wait and not seem so eager, but I can't. I type *I wish you were here right now. Kristina* and click SEND, loving the achy need his message has created inside me.

Closing my eyes, I let my hand wander to between my legs to finger myself. Ian's message has made me want to feel like he made me feel again, but then I remember his admonition to me. I want—no, need—to get off again so much, though all I can think of is him saying, "Not with me."

My phone buzzes with a message from him.

Remember, you must not touch yourself, Kristina, even if you want to. Promise?

I stop my finger's movement over my tender clit and stare at my phone in amazement. How could he know? With my hand still between my legs, I use my other hand to type out a text in return.

I promise but don't make me wait long.

My phone rings almost immediately. I know it's him, so I answer it quickly. "You're torturing me."

"I want to break you of that habit."

"There's nothing wrong with masturbation," I say with a giggle. "Cosmo says it's a healthy thing every woman should do."

"Not my woman," he answers with a smile in his voice.

"So I'm your woman? You move fast."

"Do you want me to slow down?" he asks, his voice far more serious now.

A spike of fear tears through me at the

thought of not seeing him again. That's what he means by slowing down. I know it.

I say, "No," hating that I've caused the conversation to turn like this.

He's quiet for a long time and then finally when he speaks again, the smile is back in his tone. "Good. I don't want to slow down either, Kristina. Meet me at the 79th Street entrance to Riverside Park at six tonight."

"Where are we going?"

"Somewhere you'll like."

"What should I wear?" I love the idea of surprises but figure I should be prepared.

In a voice that sends a pang of need straight to my core, he says, "Something you think I'll like."

I silently admit I barely know him, but I already know exactly what I want to wear. Something sexy yet sweet. Something that shows off my assets and hides the faults.

"Okay."

"I can't wait to see you again, Kristina."

"I can't wait either. I'll see you then."

He doesn't say goodbye. It's just that he's suddenly not there anymore and I'm alone again. I'm left wanting more of him, so I scroll back through our messages to read them over, loving how uninhibited he is and how just a few words from him can affect me so much.

The need for release returns with a vengeance, and I can't stop myself from letting my fingers get me off. I want to wait since I promised him, but it's too hard and he's gotten me too excited. There's no way I'll be able to wait another eight hours until I see him and then God knows how many hours more before I get the chance to come.

So I slide my middle finger through my slick folds and dip my fingertip inside me, dragging it up to my clit. Then with tiny circles I focus on that oh so sensitive bundle of nerves while I close my eyes and think of Ian fucking me just hours earlier. Every muscle in my body relaxes as I replay sitting on his lap riding his cock. How full I felt with him inside me. His nearly jet black eyes staring up full of lust. The taste of his tongue lashing against mine in the seconds just before he came, flooding me with his hot cum.

In just minutes, I'm dangling on the edge and know only one more gentle press of my finger will take me crashing over into the most sensual feeling there is. I think about my promise and wish I could stop, but I don't, instead sliding my fingertip over my clit one last time.

Everything around me ceases to exist. All my attention centers on my pussy and the delicious sensations my finger has created. My legs stiffen and then go weak, and I feel nothing but ecstasy as my orgasm overwhelms me.

I lie in bed unable to move, savoring the tiny aftershocks still pulsing through me. I've started every day like this since I was fifteen. At first I felt ashamed by my desires, like I shouldn't have needs like these, but over time I've accepted them. If men can jerk off every day, multiple times a day, and still be considered normal because they have urges, why can't women?

Ian simply doesn't know this is who I am. I know if he knew, he'd accept me too.

As I say that to myself, I sense my insecurities begin to file in, one by one until all I can think about is how he won't like me anymore if he finds out who I really am.

How he will leave like everyone else always has.

It happens the same way every time. They say they love me, that they can't live without me. And then slowly but surely, they do just that. By the time the press reports that another one of my relationships has ended, it's been over for a long time.

And every time I ask myself if I'm the problem. I must be, right? If every man leaves me, it must be me that's the problem. Not that I know what I'm doing wrong. I've tried to play hard to get, and I've tried giving them whatever they want. I've tried being bitchy, and I've tried being sweet. Every time it ends the same.

I just for once wish I could find someone who likes me for me. Slightly insecure, unsure of herself sometimes, but would never hurt anyone on purpose me.

Don't ruin this like always. Just let it happen. Do what that doctor told you to do. Just be yourself and let your emotions flow naturally.

But what if I do that and still another man leaves?

I EXAMINE MY look in the mirror, nervously tugging and smoothing my black jersey dress over my thighs. If only they weren't so big. And my hips. Ugh! If only they weren't so wide. Why did I have to get my mother's Scandinavian child-bearing hips? Why couldn't I have gotten my hips from my father's side of the family?

The fabric clings to every part of me I hate, but with my black knee-high boots, the dress looks terrific, so I'll stick with it. Running my hands through my hair, I let it fall in soft waves around my face and check my makeup. Thanks to my friend Marie and her makeup designer tricks, all my imperfections on my face are covered, highlighted, or diminished as perfectly as possible.

If only everything in life could be this easy.

I look at my phone and see it's almost six o'clock. Afraid I'm going to be late, I hurry toward the door, grabbing my bag and keys. Riverside Park is only a few blocks away, so I should be on time.

Ian is already there when I arrive. Dressed in dark blue jeans and a deep green sweater, he's standing next to a tree that's nearly bare of its leaves. Just a few golden ones remain. I study his body language as I approach him, hoping he isn't angry I'm late.

When he turns to face me, I see my concern was for nothing. With a smile, he smooths his dark hair off his face and says, "You look beautiful, Kristina."

All my worries melt away as his gaze slides over me and I see how much he appreciates my look. He doesn't see my big hips or thick thighs like I do. "Thank you. I love your sweater. It looks great on you."

Ian slips his hand around my waist and leans in next to my ear to whisper, "Did you leave the underwear at home like last time?"

His warm breath on my neck thrills me. Leaning back, I lower my head and feel the blush cover my cheeks. In a low voice, I answer, "Yes."

He runs his tongue over the seam of his full

lips and smiles. "Good. Let's go. I have a surprise waiting for you."

Taking my hand, he leads me away from the park and up three blocks to his apartment in a large brick building much nicer than mine. We ride up in the elevator and I fill the empty space left by his silence with talk of the weather and other meaningless topics simply because if I don't, I might burst from nerves.

Finally, I ask, "Is something wrong? You're not saying much."

He levels his dark gaze on me and stares into my eyes. "I like listening to you talk."

"I just worried there might be something wrong."

Pulling me to him, he kisses me softly and my legs get weak from how tender he is when he whispers against my lips, "How could anything be wrong?"

I taste the scotch on his tongue like the night before and wish I'd had a drink before leaving my place. At least it might have calmed my nerves a little.

His question isn't meant to be answered, and as the elevator doors open, he takes my hand to lead me down the hall to his apartment. His long fingers press against the back of my hand, and even though the hallway is beautifully decorated, all I focus on is how strong his hand feels holding mine.

"Your building is very nice," I say when we stop at his door.

He turns to look at me and nods. "I hope you like my home."

I can't imagine why I wouldn't like it since it's obviously far nicer than mine, but as we step into his apartment, I'm stunned at just how much nicer it is. At least three times the size of my tiny rooms, his seem to go on forever because of the floor to ceiling windows that line the far wall. I feel him let go of my hand, but the view out those windows mesmerizes me, and I walk toward them, eager to see what he sees every day.

"I fell in love with that view the minute I stepped into this place. The realtor couldn't stop talking about stainless steel appliances and the number of bedrooms, but I was sold the minute I looked out those windows."

I can understand why. From his living room there on the top floor, he could see practically all of the West Side and with the night sky as a backdrop, it looked like a painting deserving of being hung in a gallery.

"This must be stunning in the morning," I say as I stand as close as I can to those windows without touching them.

"I usually draw the blinds so the sun doesn't flood in, but on the rare occasion that I leave some open, it's gorgeous."

Ian wraps his arms around me, and a surge of need pushes through me straight to my core. Just his touch sends my body into overdrive so I want him even though I should be content with just standing there making small talk.

"I'm going to fuck you in front of these windows tonight. First, though, I want you to eat some of my world famous risotto."

His promise of what he plans to do to me makes a tiny whimper escape from my throat, but I try to hide my arousal with some comment about the meal he's made me. It doesn't work, though, and he says low in my ear, "I can't wait to be back inside you either, Kristina."

How would I make it through dinner when he already has me sopping wet just from a few words?

Ian guides me to a table set with fancy china dishes and crystal stemware. Two long taper candles placed in the middle of the table flicker their light over the cherry wood tabletop, the light for our meal since he dimmed the lights. He pulls my chair out and seats me like a gentleman before sitting down across from me and pouring me a glass of wine and serving me a plate of his famous risotto.

"You're going to love this," he says with pride as he hands me my dinner.

"I love that you made dinner for us. That's so sweet."

As he scoops out a spoonful of risotto onto his plate, he explains, "I didn't know if we'd be mobbed by photographers if we went out to a restaurant, so I thought I'd surprise you with my favorite dish."

Raising his wine glass, he says with a devilish smile, "To having all my favorites tonight."

I smile and raise my glass, admiring how handsome he looks in the candlelight. "To favorites."

The risotto tastes as good as he'd promised, and I eat every last bite of it on my plate. In contrast to his earlier promise of having me against those huge windows that look out over the city, he talks about where he learned to cook and how much he enjoys making his favorite foods when he has the chance. I make a few comments, but I can't help feel confused. We switched so quickly from talking about fucking so all the world could see to how risotto takes so long to make because of how the stock has to be added slowly that I don't know how to react.

"Is everything okay?" he asks as he clears the

plates from the table.

I want to say that this all seems so domestic compared to our time together the night before. Not that I don't like a man cooking for me, but I guess I just expected something different. Instead I just smile and shake my head.

"No. Dinner was lovely."

"You seem quiet since we got here."

He's so observant compared to other men I've been with that I forget he notices things. Since all I'd done was pretty much chatter on about everything under the sun yesterday and this evening as we were coming up in the elevator, I must seem very different now.

I take a drink of my wine. "Your apartment is very nice."

Ian smiles and stands up from the table. He walks around behind me and leans over to kiss me on the neck. "You said that before, Kristina. Why don't you tell me what's wrong?"

God, his deep voice feels like it's traveling right to the center of my being. I close my eyes and say quietly, "I guess I'm just a little nervous."

As he gently fastens his hand on the front of my neck, he says in a voice so low I can barely hear him, "You look beautiful tonight. This dress accentuates all my favorite parts of your body. Did you know that?"

"No. I was afraid it make me look too hippy and showed off my worst part," I reluctantly admit as my hands move to cover my legs, afraid he'll agree with me or worse, say nothing.

He remains silent but takes my hand to lead me over to the windows. Standing behind me again, he places his hand back on my throat and nuzzles just under my ear, saying in a deep voice, "When I eat your pussy in a few minutes, anyone in that building there will be able to see your entire body because you'll be naked in front of all these windows. Do you know what they'll see?"

I lean back to melt into his body and answer, "No."

"They'll see a gorgeous woman being worshipped by a man who can't help but adore her. They won't see a body part. You're beautiful because of the sum of your parts, not for one part alone."

Closing my eyes, I let his wonderful words sink into my brain. All those times that I'd been so self-conscious about some part of my body, all I'd wanted to hear was something like that and no one has ever said it to me. Until now.

CHAPTER FOUR

Kristina

H E COULD COMMAND me to do anything in the world, and after hearing those words I wouldn't refuse him. As I stand there looking out at the city in front of me, I don't want to refuse him. I don't know if it's the way he phrases things or the sound of his voice when he says them, but his words enchant me like no one's ever have before.

Ian wraps his arms around me, holding me tightly to him, and says low in my ear, "There's nothing sexier than a woman who knows how to give herself to a man, Kristina."

I want to say yes, that I wish I could be that kind of woman, but I push my insecurities down and remain silent. Maybe if I don't say anything, he won't see that I'm really not that woman he finds so desirable.

Not yet, anyway.

But I want to be that. I want to be the kind of

woman who turns him on like no other.

His mouth presses against the tender skin just below my right ear and lingers there, sending ribbons of desire winding through my body. My gaze focuses on a light in an apartment in the building across the way as Ian's hands slowly slide my dress up to the top of my thighs, revealing my garter belt and bare pussy.

"Do you think he can see us?" he asks with a devilish lilt to his voice, as if having someone watch us is exactly what he hopes for.

"I don't know," I say quietly while his fingers tease the skin where my body meets my legs. Then a thought occurs to me. Has Ian put on this show with other women before? I don't want to think he has, but the idea quickly begins to grow in my mind, making me tense up when he slides his finger through my wet folds.

"Something wrong, Kristina?"

I hear in his voice a displeasure that upsets me even more than the thought of him with other women. Shaking my head, I whisper, "No."

His hand leaves my body, a sign he doesn't believe my lie. Walking around to face me, he stands in front of me, shielding me from the potential prying eyes of the person across the street. He stares with those dark eyes studying my expression and smiles. "Better?"

Smiling, I nod my head as he cradles my face in his hands, making me feel cherished and important. "Thank you."

"Tell me, did you obey my command not to touch yourself this morning?"

My heart pounds against my chest as my brain plays tug of war with itself. Do I lie again, only to be caught, or do I tell him the truth, surely upsetting our time together? His gaze zeroes in on my eyes, and I'm sure he sees right through me. I have no choice. I have to tell the truth.

Fearing I'm about to ruin our night, I take a deep breath and bite my lip nervously. His eyes never veer from mine, silently commanding me once again to obey him. I can't stand up to his scrutiny and look away as I give my answer.

"No."

I feel entirely alone as I stare out the window, wishing the possible person across the street was there so I could pretend to speak to him to ease my tension as I wait for Ian to say something. One syllable and I fear it's revealed who I am and made him dislike me. I can't help but anticipate his next words, praying they aren't him telling me to leave.

He remains silent, but I can sense his stare on my cheek. The room feels like all the air has been sucked out, and I can't help but close my eyes to avoid the truth.

This is why everyone leaves. Who would want to be with someone who can't even do the simplest thing to show she can be trusted?

"Look at me, Kristina."

His words sound clipped, like he's working to keep his temper even. I don't immediately obey this command either, too scared to turn my head and face what will happen.

"Look at me now."

There's no mistaking his tone. He's angry. Quietly, I say, "I'm sorry," and hang my head.

His hand gently grips my jaw and turns my head so I have no choice but to face him. Opening my eyes, I see his dark eyes gleaming and his mouth hitched up into a smile.

"I knew you wouldn't do as I asked. Maybe it was unfair to make that demand," he says as he pushes my hair behind my left ear.

"You aren't angry with me?"

Ian shakes his head. "No. It's more important that you told me the truth. I need to know I can trust you. Making you ignore your natural urge to feel good wasn't the right way to find that out. I'm sorry."

"You can trust me, Ian. I promise. I'm sorry I couldn't stop myself, but your texts got me so excited..." I let my sentence trail off as I watched the smile slide from his face. Had I said something wrong?

"I want to ask you something, Kristina."

"Anything. You can ask me whatever you want."

"Will you be my muse?"

His question registers in my brain, but I can't understand how I could be his muse. "What do you mean? How could someone like me be a muse for an historical fiction writer?"

Ian traces his fingertip along the swell of my lower lip and leans in to kiss me softly. "I've begun to write something new, different from the books I usually write."

"What would I do as your muse?"

His eyes sparkle as he speaks. "You'd inspire me. That's what a muse does."

"How could I inspire you? What kind of book is this?"

"It's an erotic story. It came to me one night after watching a movie." His voice drops and he adds, "One of your movies."

I can't help but feel enchanted as I stand there listening to him confess he began writing something sensual after watching me. I kiss him softly on the lips and whisper, "I'd be honored to be your muse, Ian."

His smile thrills me, but then his expression

changes to one far more serious. "I need you to promise me to keep this our secret, Kristina. No one else can know."

"Okay. Why?"

"Think of it like nude photos of yourself. While in context they might be tasteful and beautiful, if they got into the wrong hands, your career might suffer because of it."

"Are you worried your fans wouldn't like this new book?"

"Yes, so I'm going to be writing under a pseudonym. I don't want you hurt by this either, though, so unless you can promise this will remain a secret between us and only us, we can't go any further."

I sense him backing away even as he stands in front of me. I don't want to stop what we're doing. Never before have I felt so sexy and desirable with a man.

"No. I promise not to tell a soul. Just between you and me."

He strokes my cheek with the back of his hand and kisses me on the tip of my nose. "Good. Now about our friend across the way…"

Before I can ask what he means, Ian lowers himself to his knees and slides his palms over my thighs to the top of my garter belt. His soft touch thrills me. I close my eyes as he leans forward to press his mouth to my sex and his tongue flattens against my sensitive skin, sending a jolt of need to my core.

Leaning back, he looks up at me. "I'll let you stay dressed while I eat your pussy for him, but after you come the first time, I want him to see all of you as I take you right here."

Nothing in what he says asks permission or allows for any doubt on my part. I know this. If his words didn't make it clear, the look in his eyes does. He's hungry for me—as hungry for me as I am for him. It makes me want to please him even more.

"What if I want him to see you going down on me too?" I ask, almost daring him to deny me.

The sparkle in his eyes that's been there since he asked me to be his muse flashes the purest look of need I've ever seen and he says in a voice low and deep, "Take the dress off, Kristina."

I slide my dress over my head and then I'm standing in full view of anyone nearby in just my bra, garter belt, and stockings. Ian licks his lips and grins, but says nothing, instead grabbing the backs of my thighs and pulling me roughly to him. Without pause, he returns to devour my wet pussy, his tongue sending strings of delight through me as he flicks my needy clit.

The urge to close my eyes is strong, but I

don't want to hide behind them and pretend. I want to be the sexual creature Ian sees me as—his beautiful and erotic muse. When he lifts my leg and slings it over his shoulder to bury his tongue deep inside my cunt, I dig my fingers into his collarbone to hang on, loving how I feel there on display.

His fingers spread me wide, and Ian sucks my clit between his lips. Just as I think I can't handle any more, I feel his teeth bite down gently and I'm lost. My leg buckles as my orgasm rushes over me, and every inch of my body feels like it's flying. I sense Ian's hands holding me up, but I can't feel anything but the complete and utter ecstasy of coming from the incredible sensations his mouth created in me.

"I bet he loved seeing that," Ian whispers as he plants tiny kisses along my inner thigh.

Looking down, I smile at how sexy he looks kneeling in front of me. Tousling his hair with my fingers, I want more. I want to feel him inside me, stretching me to take all of him.

"Come here."

Instead of standing, he pulls me down onto the floor and kisses me, his lips still wet from going down on me. I taste myself on his tongue as it teases mine. Moaning his name, I fumble with his zipper as I try to free his cock.

"Not yet," he warns as he moves my hand away.

"Why?" I don't mean to whine, but it comes out like that because I want more.

"Sit on my lap and straddle my legs."

I do as he tells me to and quickly realize what he has in mind when he removes my bra. Tugging his hair harder than I should, I pull him toward one nipple, and he roughly takes it into his mouth. He sucks hard, making my tender skin pebble instantly and my pussy run wet with the need to come again. I instinctively rock against him and feel his hard cock beneath his pants as I grind against the full length of him.

"You like it rough?" he asks as he leans back away from me.

"No, not usually," I answer as he pinches my excited nipple, sending a jolt of pleasure straight to my clit.

"You do with me."

Needy for more, I pull his hair hard to direct his mouth to my other breast, eager for his lips to repeat their delicious torture. He sucks it hard, his teeth sinking into the base of my nipple harder than before. His hands squeeze my tender flesh, one surrounding where his mouth is and the other pinching my other nipple so both get to enjoy his attention.

His touch borders on pain I'm not sure I can withstand, but I stop myself from crying out, wanting it more than I want him to stop. Just as I'm sure I can't take anymore, he slides his right hand down to my pussy and thrusts two fingers inside me. They graze a spot only he seems to find, and I whimper his name softly.

My nipple pops out of his mouth as he turns his focus to his fingers' movement, and instantly I miss the feel of his lips and teeth on me. He sees the loss on my face, and smiling a devilish grin, says, "My girl definitely likes it rough. We'll get back to that later, though."

"Later?" I ask, disappointment covering me as he slides his fingers out of me. "Why?"

"We have a show to put on for that man over there. We wouldn't want to let him down, would we?"

His mouth slants over mine in a kiss so passionate and deep that he nearly takes my breath away. This show excites him.

"You really like this thing with others seeing us, don't you?"

Ian draws his finger from my lips down between my breasts and nods. "I do. You do too."

I can't deny that something about a stranger in the dark watching us excites me. I've never been an exhibitionist, but with Ian I want to do things I've never considered. What does that man look like, though? Is he old? Young? Short? Who is he?

Standing, Ian pulls me to my feet and kisses me long and hard, his tongue forcing its way into my mouth play with mine. He turns me around to face the window so he's standing behind me and drags his fingertip up my wet slit.

"I want him to see all of you when I fuck your tight cunt."

"Yes," I whisper as I hear his pants drop to the floor and feel his hard cock nudge my ass. "Don't wait, Ian."

He rears back away from me and for a moment I'm alone waiting to feel him again. Then his hand is on my throat as he rams his cock into me and says in my ear, "Tell me how you feel, Kristina. Tell me everything."

"Full…hot…don't stop."

"Never. I need to feel you around me."

Ian thrusts his hips forward, stretching me for a long moment before he slowly slides out of me, leaving my body needy for more.

"Faster…please…"

My pleas are met with him slamming into me over and over, the swollen head of his cock rubbing that spot that feels like heaven. I come as his hand tightens around my throat and he says,

"That's one. You want more?"

"Yes," I say breathlessly. My body aches for more.

Ian fucks me until I come twice more, but still he doesn't come. I wonder what's wrong, but he seems happy and content, whispering in my ear, "Ready to change the show for our friend?"

I turn to see him smiling and nod my agreement. "I want him to see you come."

"Then down on your knees."

Lowering myself to the wood floor, I feel the hardness press against my knees and instantly wish Ian had wanted something else. Never as big a fan of going down on men as other women are, it simply isn't what I consider my best position, and all I can think of as I stare up at him is that he'll be as disappointed with my performance as I usually am.

"Is something wrong, Kristina?"

I shake my head and press a smile onto my lips. "No."

Ian crouches down in front of me and takes my face in his hands. "Don't be scared. It's no different than what we were just doing. I want you to enjoy yourself."

My brows knit, and I know my face shows the concern filling me with dread. "I just—"

"Don't worry. There's no way a beautiful

mouth like yours won't make me feel more incredible than I've ever felt before."

"Okay."

He stands and as he winks at me like a sign that we're in this together, he wraps his hand around his cock and feeds it to me, slowly sliding it into my waiting mouth. His skin tastes musky and has a hint of saltiness to it, and suddenly I realize I'm tasting me on him. My eyes open wide and for a moment I think about telling him I can't do this.

I've never done this before after a man's been inside me. A mixture of emotions fill my mind, but then I look up and see him staring down at me and I want to make him happy. To make him feel as good as he's made me feel tonight. So I push my fear and nerves aside and do just that.

Make him happy.

His cock is long and thicker than anyone I've been with, so it doesn't take long for my jaw to ache. I can only take about half his length into my mouth, but I work the bottom half with my hand, pumping his soft skin as I suck the top and head. His moans tell me I'm doing it right, but I can't help but wish I was better at this.

His hands slide through my hair and roughly tighten into fists. Pain skitters across my scalp as he tugs my head down onto his cock. My eyes closed now, I hear him say, "Let me see what that pretty mouth can really do."

He directs me to go as fast as he wants, easing my head down slowly until nearly all of his cock disappears into my mouth, and then he pulls my head up quickly so he nearly pops out from between my lips. Over and over, he does this as he groans how good it feels and how much he loves the feel of my mouth on him.

I feel his balls tighten near my hand and he tugs my hair so hard tears come to my eyes. About to come, he slides nearly all of his cock out of my mouth until just a few inches are left inside me and groans, "Take it all, baby."

His cock throbbing, he floods my mouth, and the hot liquid rolls down the back of my throat. I've never finished going down on a man, always choosing to stop before they came, so this is the first time I'm tasting anyone. The experience is strangely empowering as I look up and see Ian with his eyes closed and a look of complete ecstasy covering his face.

In that moment, I forget about the possible audience across the street and focus entirely on the man there with me. For the first time, it's just Ian and me, and I want more than anything to know I've made him happy.

CHAPTER FIVE

Ian

KRISTINA GENTLY SNORES next to me, easing me out of a sound sleep as my brain tries to figure out why there'd be a noise in my room. I'm not used to having someone in my bed, but as I open my eyes all the way to watch her, I like the feeling of having her there.

I push her brown hair off her face and see her mouth turns down into a tiny pout as she sleeps. It reminds me of every picture I've ever seen of babies sleeping. I reach out and softly touch her bottom lip, tracing the softness of her skin as I remember the pleasure her mouth gave me hours earlier.

Her confession afterward that she'd never finished a man surprised me, but that soon changed to a sense of pride that she'd been willing to do that for me. She's surprised me with her ability to be so forthcoming. Few women are that way, in my experience, and the ones who are quickly show themselves to be truthful more to gain something than to simply share a part of themselves.

But not Kristina.

Her candor charms me more than I thought I could be. I can't help but want her because of her openness. What began as a fascination—an obsession borne of infatuation—has grown to more far quicker than any of my other addictions, but unlike with them, I haven't thought even once to stop myself from falling.

She has no idea of the depth of my desire for her. No doubt to her I'm just a typical male who's wasted no time getting in her pants. I don't deny that part of my attraction to her, but there's more. The need to hear her soft voice, to see her blue eyes as she looks at me like she cares—the need to have these things around me begins the moment I wake up.

This is the life of an addict. I know this. I also know if I told her what I really am she'd likely run away and never want to come back. For now, all I want is her, but the time may come that I want alcohol or junk more than her.

Who am I kidding? It's not a matter of if but when. I know this, but as I look over at her sleeping so sweetly next to me, her mouth in a tiny pout that makes me want to take her in my arms and never let her go, I want to believe that this time will be different.

"Did I wake you?" she asks as she rubs the sleep from her eyes.

"No," I say, shaking my head, happy to lie to save her any amount of embarrassment.

"Is it late?"

"I don't know. I didn't check the time. I was just watching you sleep."

Kristina buries her head in the pillow and mumbles, "I snored, didn't I?"

"Not too bad. I had to get up anyway."

Giggling, she picks her head up and I see she's blushing. "I'm so sorry. I snore like a lumberjack, or at least that's what my sister always says. She refused to sleep in a room with me when we were teenagers."

"No, not a lumberjack. More like an adorable little saw cutting through wood. Like something in a cartoon."

"That's still awful!" she says with a smile. "Sorry about that. If I do it again, just roll me over. That usually works."

"I'll keep that in mind."

"So not sexy, right? Actress Kristina Richards snores like an old man. I can see the cover of The Enquirer now."

"I promise it's our secret. I won't tell another

living soul."

She touches my shoulder and traces her finger down over my collarbone. "That's two secrets now. I had no idea you were so cloak and dagger."

"I'm like the CIA—full of secrets," I say with a smile, my answer far more truthful than she can know.

"I think I like that. A man of mystery. Sounds sexy."

Her sweetness continues to charm me, even first thing in the morning before I've had my coffee. Is she always this cute when she wakes up?

I want to tell her nothing would make me happier than just lying there in bed with her all day, but that would probably come across as too much so early in the relationship. That's the kind of thing people say after they've moved in together, not on the second date.

Is it really just the second time we've been together? It feels like I've known her for ages.

"You're pretty quiet. Are you one of those people who hate mornings?"

"Not really. I'm just too dependent on coffee at this time of day. You're not like that?"

Kristina shakes her head and smiles. "No. I don't drink coffee. I'm a tea person. They say tea has more caffeine than coffee, though, so it's the same addiction. I'm guessing you don't have any tea here, though."

I stretch the sleep from my limbs and think if I have any tea in my kitchen. As someone who doesn't drink it, there wouldn't be much reason to have any, but I think my mother might have left some one time when she came to visit me. All of this runs through my head surprisingly fast for this time of day, and I nod. "Maybe. We can check when we finally get up."

A shy smile spreads across her beautiful mouth. "Oh. We're not getting up now?"

"No. I'm not ready to leave this bed just yet."

"Got anything in mind?"

"Yeah."

As I roll her over on her stomach, I can only think of one thing I want to do.

AFTER KRISTINA LEAVES, I get ready for a full day of planning this new project that more than ever has my attention. Silk, as I'm calling it, is the story of a woman who fights her addiction to heroin through her other addiction, sex. The main character, Kate Silk, is a famous actress who wants to be known as more than just some Hollywood starlet gone wrong. Her story is much like every famous star who's fallen on hard times, but she's determined to be the exception to the rule.

I sit down in front of my laptop and let the ideas flow from my fingers. Far quicker than when I brainstorm for my historical fiction, the story begins to take shape right there in front of me on the screen. Kate's appearance, her backstory, the conflict all come so easily, but then I see why.

They're Kristina.

Even though I know little about her life before we met, except for her work in films, because I still refuse to cyberstalk her instead of gleaning the information the old fashioned way— through conversation and serious moments together—I imagine the details so the story comes alive. Eventually, I'll find out about Kristina's past, but for now, what I create for Kate's past will work just fine.

Six hours later, I sit back proud of my work and satisfied with how Silk is shaping up. I've spent all day in Kate Silk's world, one I know all too well. I didn't plot out the parts about her addictions. I don't need to. I've lived it for so long that story is part of me, part of every day of my life.

For now, Kristina is my addiction, and after so many hours without her, I need to see her. I call her and just the sound of her voice eases the edginess I began to feel hours ago.

"Hi Ian! Did you miss me?" she asks playfully.

"I did. Am I seeing you tonight?"

"Another dinner planned or something different?"

"I'd like to tell you about the book you've inspired. I can order Chinese, if you like, and we can talk about it."

"I'd love that! Say eight?"

I quickly calculate how long until I can see her. Four hours. I can make it that long.

"Eight's good. Do you want me to get some wine for you? All I have here is scotch."

"I'll tell you what. I'll bring the wine, and you get the Chinese. I love General Tso's chicken. Not very Chinese, but the place a few blocks from you tastes great."

"Then it'll be you, me, and the General for dinner."

There's a pause in our conversation and then she asks, "Should I dress any particular way? I don't want to be underdressed if we're going somewhere."

"Wear whatever you love. I want you to be comfortable here."

"Okay. Eight o'clock with you and the General. It's a date. I'll see you then, Ian."

I PACE THE room back and forth, each time

checking to see if the minute hand on the clock has moved any closer to eight. I've been doing this for thirty minutes, unable to keep my mind from thinking about her. This is obsession. This is addiction.

This is me.

The knock on my door makes my heart leap in my chest, but I stop myself from racing to the door and flinging it open to see if it's Kristina or the delivery man with our Chinese food. Neither one of them would understand my behavior.

Slowly, with measured steps, I make it to the door and open it to find her standing there smiling up at me. I want to take her in my arms and hold her to me. I don't only because I know she wouldn't understand.

Don't want to come on too strong. Go easy at first or you'll scare her away.

The words repeat in my mind as I welcome her in and escort her to the kitchen to open the wine. She's talking about something going on down on the street, but I'm focused on her white sweater that appears to have been made especially for her. It clings to her body perfectly, hugging her breasts as if to showcase them.

She's dressed this way for me. The fact makes keeping my hands off her next to impossible, but as she continues to explain something about a group of people in front of my building, I work to not touch her so soon, stuffing my hands into my pockets to hold myself back.

"I think they recognized me, but thankfully, something happened in the street and I was able to slip inside without having to wait for you to let me up. Thank God for your doorman."

I absentmindedly answer and smile even though I have no idea what she's talking about. Taking the wine bottle from her hands, I find the corkscrew and open it for her. Pouring her a glass, I hand it to her and receive one of her beautiful smiles in return.

"No drink for you?" she asks as she looks around for my glass.

"Not yet. I'm content as I am for now."

Kristina takes a sip of her wine and places the glass on the counter as she licks her lips. I watch her tongue moisten them like it's the most interesting act I've ever seen.

"Ian, is something wrong? You're staring at me and not saying much."

"No," I answer and shake my head.

"Okay." She steps toward me and kisses me, whispering against my mouth, "I thought about you today."

I taste the sweetness of the wine on her lips as my tongue slides into her mouth. It's fresh and natural, not syrupy, and it dances across my taste buds. This is what I'll think of when I want to remember how her kiss tastes.

Her fingers caress the tips of my ears, tickling me, and I pull her mouth to mine in a deeper kiss that makes my cock stiffen. I want her right there against the counter in my kitchen. I push my hand under her sweater and cup her breast through her bra. Under my touch, her nipple tightens into an excited peak, and I squeeze it hard between my thumb and forefinger, loving the sound of her whimpering into my mouth.

Reaching down, I slide my hand under her purple skirt to find the black tights she's wearing only go to the tops of her thighs. Above them, all I feel is soft skin because she's doesn't have panties or even a garter belt on. The need to be inside her makes my chest tighten with need, and I break our kiss to take a breath.

"I almost gave the whole world a show on my way here when a gust of wind blew my skirt up," she tells me with a cute smile, not knowing how jealous the idea of other people seeing her like that makes me.

She presses her body to mine and tilts her hips to feel the hardness of my cock. I know I should wait—that I shouldn't want to fuck her every time I see her—but just her being near me makes my body crave her. Inching my fingers up over her hip, I feel the smooth skin of her bare pussy and want to bury my face in her.

One finger slides over her clit, and I lick my lips at how incredible she feels. "I love how wet you are for me already."

Kristina moans and whispers hoarsely, "When I thought about you today, it was of how good it feels when you're inside me."

An ache comes over me when I hear those words, like the only way to make it go away is to bury myself balls deep in her and fuck the pain away. I unzip my pants and my cock practically springs out, ready and willing like the rest of me.

Lifting her, I thrust once and I'm inside her, loving the feel of her wet cunt around my cock. Her hands cling to my neck, and I grip her hips to absorb my stabs into her body. The need to come, to make her come, overtakes me so I can think of nothing else. I press her against the wall and fuck her hard, every plunge into her body another attempt to sate my need for her.

She meets my thrusts with her own, rocking her hips against me as she moans for me to fuck her harder. My hips hurt and my back aches, but I don't stop. I can't stop. I need the release she can give me. I need to make her come.

We hear the knock at the door and we look

into each other's eyes, the two of us silently questioning whether the other one will stop. I shake my head and continue pounding into her, and she closes her eyes. I feel her body just seconds away from surrender.

She feels it too. In my ear, she sobs, "Don't stop. Please don't stop, Ian. I'm almost there."

I couldn't stop even if I wanted to. My body demands a reprieve from the cravings I've had all day, and Kristina is the only one who can give it to me. Another knock at the door drowns out our moans for a moment, and I say in her ear just as I feel her body begin to tighten around me, "Come for me. Give me all you have."

Her teeth clamp down on my shoulder as her orgasm explodes through her, sending streaks of pain across my back and neck, but I don't care. She could bite me to the bone. My body is too busy rejoicing in the feeling of her cunt milking my cock for me to give a fuck about anything but the perfect pleasure she brings out in me. I come hard into her, flooding her body until it streams down between us.

Panting, she says sweetly, "The Chinese delivery guy probably left."

"Unless I can go to the door just like this, I don't care."

Kristina kisses me tenderly and hugs me.

Pressing her lips to my ear, she says quietly, "I want to say I didn't mean for this to happen again, but since I didn't wear anything under my skirt, I guess that would be a lie."

I lean back and look up at her. "Are we going too fast?"

For a moment, she's silent, but then she says, "I should say yes. I know that. I know we should know all sorts of things before we get to this point. My friends say I jump into relationships too fast. But I don't care. I like the way I feel when I'm with you."

I lie and say what I know I should say. "Just tell me if you want to slow down. We can take this slower."

She shakes her head and a tiny frown mars her beautiful face still covered in an after sex glow. "No. I didn't mean it that way. I love the way you can't seem to keep your hands off me. It makes me feel beautiful."

"You are beautiful."

Her smile in response to my compliment thrills me. I kiss her and slowly lower her to the floor. She looks down at my still hard cock and winks at me. "I'll check to see if the Chinese is still nearby. You get yourself straightened up."

I hand her the money and zip my cock back into my cum-soaked pants as I watch her walk toward the door and love the view of her from behind. Shaking my head, I try to focus on something else. I've just finished fucking her not five minutes before and all I can think of is doing it again.

Kristina somehow finds the delivery guy and closes the door, a bag containing our dinner in her arms. "He looked at me like he knew exactly what we were doing while he was out in the hallway. I gave him a big tip."

Taking the food from her hands, I kiss her and run my tongue over her lips. "As long as that's all you gave him."

"He's not my type. I prefer my men tall, lean, with dark hair and eyes darker than I've ever seen in another person."

I smile at her description of me as I unload the General Tso's Chicken and Moo Shu Pork from the bag. "Anything else you like in your men?"

She wraps her arms around my waist and presses her cheek to my back. "I like it when they know just the right words to say."

"I guess it's a good thing I'm an author then."

Pressing a light kiss onto my cheek, she snatches her food out from in front of me and walks toward the table. "I guess so. Are we eating in here?"

I think about how she likes what I do, even though what I write isn't usually sexy. "No, let's sit on the couch and eat. Then I can tell you about the story."

Peeking her head back into the kitchen, she says, "I can't wait. I'm dying to hear what a story inspired by me sounds like."

"Patience, grasshopper. All in good time," I joke as I follow her into the living room and sit down next to her, happier than I've been in too long.

CHAPTER SIX

Ian

K RISTINA SNUGGLES UP against my side and coos, "I can't eat another bite. I'm all General Tso'd out."

"I was Moo Shu'd about ten minutes ago. I should have stopped eating, but it's so good. Sure you don't want a taste? I've got a forkful or so left."

Shaking her head, she says, "No. I'm stuffed. I'm going to struggle to keep my eyes open after eating so much."

I put the fork down and lean back on the couch, holding her as my back settles in against the leather. "If the story was one of my usual ones, I could understand that."

She looks up at me with worry in her eyes. "No, that's not what I meant at all. I love all your work. I mean that." I hear in her voice the fear that she's offended me.

"It's okay. Except for other writers, this part

isn't the exciting stuff anyway. I could understand if you didn't find it very interesting."

Kissing me on the side of my face, she repeats that she doesn't find my work boring. Even if she doesn't mean what she says, it's still nice to hear it.

"I want to know about all your writing, Ian. That you can string words together like you do to make such fantastic books amazes me. People always think actors are the great ones, but they only deliver the lines. It's the people who write them who are truly the great ones."

I turn and kiss her on the top of the head. "We'll see if you still think that after I tell you about this new story."

She brings her legs up underneath her and sits up straight beside me. "I'm all ears."

"I guess I have a confession to make. I began to write this before we met."

"I thought I was your muse for this, though?"

"You are. I got the idea for this book after watching your movies," I say quietly and then wait for her response.

"You did? Something from one of my movies made you want to write this book?"

I look into her eyes and tell her the truth. "Not something. You. You made me want to write this book."

"Me?"

"Yeah. You."

I see in her expression what I've said confuses her, so I try to explain my creative process without putting her to sleep for real. "You see, for a writer, ideas can come from just about anything. A song. A scene I see outside the cab as I head to a friend's house. A movie. That's what happened. I was watching one of yours the other night and the story just came to me."

This isn't exactly the truth. I know this. But telling someone I became obsessed with her after watching every single movie she's ever made isn't as romantic as they make it sound in romance books.

"So my acting inspired you?"

I nod, choosing not to explain anymore since I'd probably say too much and ruin the moment.

"That's so wonderful. I always wonder how my work affects others. Usually I think it doesn't much at all. People watch the films and want to meet me, but it's mainly because they like how I look. But this shows me that there are people out there who see more than just the outside of me. That the way I play a part can show more of the inside of me. Which movie was it?"

Her question makes my heart skip a beat. I can't remember what movie it was. I watched every single one back to back for hours on end, but even at this moment I can't say what any one of them was about and certainly don't know their names.

"I'm terrible with remembering names and titles," I lie. An author who can't remember details. Not very believable. "I think it was the one that was the remake of The Misfits."

"Oh, I loved that part! Do you know Marilyn Monroe played it first, alongside Clark Gable?" she asks, her eyes wide with enthusiasm.

"I do. That's probably why I remembered."

I don't want to dampen her passion for talking about her job, but a few more questions about why I enjoy her acting and it will become clear I'm not a fan of the acting so much of her. I wait until she says a few more things about the film, and then I gently try to move her back toward talking about the book.

"You're a lot like the main character in Silk. I think being with you has influenced me a lot already." It's a tepid lie, but there's some truth in it.

"What's the story about?"

I choose my words carefully because I've just said she's like a heroin addict who uses sex to suppress her urges to get high. "Kate Silk is sensitive and gentle, but she finds it difficult to deal with a lot of daily life because of that. She's beautiful and giving."

"You see me as sensitive and giving?" Kristina asks with tears in her eyes.

Kissing the tip of her nose, I smile. "Of course. Why wouldn't I?"

"Because I'm a Hollywood actress. All people generally see of me is the outside."

"Well, as an author, I see things other people might not."

"So what is her story, this sensitive and giving woman?" she asks and I can't avoid telling her the real plot.

"She's a recovering addict," I say quietly. "Every day she deals with the cravings her want for heroin force on her. The only way she finds she can master them is with sex."

Kristina's quiet for a long moment and finally says, "I bet it's way deeper than that, but you don't want to tell me because you think it would bore me. I bet she fights against those cravings every minute of the day and sex isn't just a physical act to her but a way to push down the need for something that hurts her."

Her blue eyes are filled with emotion as she speaks. I can't help but be impressed with how much she seems to understand addiction. "Have you ever been addicted to anything?"

Shaking her head, she smiles meekly. "No, but my old therapist used to tell me all the time that I'm addicted to people. I don't think she's right, but she says that's why all my relationships fail. Because I get addicted to the other person and he doesn't get addicted to me back."

Sounds like typical psychobabble bullshit therapists like to spew. Perhaps a person can be addicted to the feelings someone creates in them or the way they treat them, but addicted to a person? Bullshit.

"I wouldn't listen to her," I say with a smile. "She doesn't sound like she knows much about addiction, to be honest."

"Do you?"

Nodding, I wonder how much I should tell Kristina about who I really am. If she spends enough time with me, she's going to find out. It always returns like some ugly demon I push to the background but never really goes away. I could just lie and tell her about the drinking, but that's only something I use to calm the pangs of need for the real thing I'm addicted to that wash over me most days and threaten to drown me on the worst of them.

"Yeah."

Touching my arm in a gesture of sympathy, she says, "If you don't want to talk about it, Ian, you don't have to. Don't feel like you have to talk about anything you don't want to with me."

This is one of the problems with a relationship moving at warp speed. The sex twenty-four-seven is great, but along with that real life intrudes with all its ugliness and reality.

"It's not exactly what someone wants to hear the third time they're with someone, right?"

"Are you worried if you tell me something bad about yourself that I won't want to see you anymore?" she asks in a voice so sweet I can't help but want to confess everything about myself to her.

"It's not just bad. That's the problem."

Kristina turns my face toward her and kisses me softly. "There's nothing you can tell me that would make me not want to see you, Ian. Do your worst."

As much as I want to believe her, I know the truth. It never leaves me. No matter how much I may look like the successful author my agent promotes me as or the man Kristina thinks I am, the truth is I'm an addict, pure and simple. An addict who when he isn't snorting junk up his nose searches for something else to become addicted to so he doesn't fuck up his life again.

"I never did any drugs in high school, strangely enough since that's when so many people are introduced to them. Even in college, all I did was smoke some pot. Nothing big. It wasn't until much later that I had my first taste of heroin."

She says nothing and I know I should stop. If I go much further, she'll know what I am and will probably want to leave and never see me again. I know this and still I keep going.

"It was my first editor who introduced me to heroin. I was so naïve back then. I thought the only way you could do heroin was shooting up, so when he first asked me if I'd ever done it, I was horrified. I hate needles, so there was no way I would've ever used any drug that required sticking myself with something."

Kristina says nothing, but her hold on my arm steadily grows stronger as I continue confessing who I am.

"The first time I did it all I felt was relaxed for around a half hour. I didn't think much of it and couldn't imagine what he was talking about when he said it would make me feel better than I'd ever felt before. Then everything changed. One minute all I felt was relaxed and almost sleepy and then the next minute I was flying. The rush was incredible. It was at that point that I knew just what he meant."

"Why did he give you drugs?"

"I was a mess with my first book. I knew how to write, but I didn't know how to handle everything that happens after you get the book written. People think authors get the words down on the page in some kind of magical way and then the book shows up in stores ready for them to read. It doesn't happen like that. What really happens is an author writes the book and then it goes into edits where it gets torn apart and put back together again."

"That sounds painful."

"It can be. We writers get very attached to our work. Our words are our creations, our babies. But then editors come in and carve into those babies. Their job is to make our work better, but it can hurt if you're not used to it. I wasn't with my first book. I'd gotten an agent with what I'd written and she'd gotten me a publishing deal, so I couldn't imagine what the editor would want to change. I was in for a rude awakening."

Kristina leans her head against my shoulder. "I like thinking of that guy who was so naïve. He sounds cute."

I look down at her and chuckle at her description of me back then. "I was such a newbie. I got my edits back and fell apart. The editor had to actually sit with me and calm me down, and that's when he gave me my first taste of heroin. It did what it was supposed to. I calmed down and then I felt better than I'd ever felt before in my life."

My story makes my addiction far more romantic than it actually is. Beginnings always are. It's that time after the initial wonder and excitement that shows what something really is.

"Were you immediately addicted to it?"

I think back to the days following that night I snorted heroin with Robert and remember liking how I felt but not feeling some overwhelming need to feel like that again. "No. I liked feeling that way, but I think if I never had it again I wouldn't have missed it."

"But you did do it again. Why?"

"I had more edits to do. That's another misconception about books. Edits aren't something that just happen in a day or so and then the book's done. There are rounds of edits and sometimes they feel like they go on forever. So every time I got overwhelmed, my editor made sure I had something to calm me down and get me to a place where I wasn't overwhelmed."

"Why would he do that?"

"He's an addict and knew it would help me, so I guess he figured misery loves company. I got the book's edits completed and it went on to be a huge seller. But I was addicted by the time the book hit the bestseller lists."

"Do you still do heroin?" she asks and I hear what she can't mask. The judgment. The fear.

She has every right to be afraid. Anyone who lets a junkie into their life should be afraid. We wreck things.

I answer truthfully. "No. Do I want to? All the time. More than you can know. But I don't. I've been through rehab three times. After the second time, things got better for a while. For a long time, I didn't touch it. But then something triggered whatever it is inside me that wants that feeling and I went hard into it. That's when I went to rehab the third time and got clean. I've been off it for eight months now, and I just finished a book without it for the first time ever."

She kisses my cheek, but I know what I just told her is probably making her wonder if she should run away as fast as she can. She should, but I hope she won't.

"And that book just hit the New York Times bestsellers list, didn't it?"

I smile. I'm proud of that book for more than just the writing. "It did. That book showed me I can do it without turning to putting that shit up my nose."

"Ian, I don't understand why you'd want to write about a character who struggles with heroin addiction. Won't it make you think about how much you want it again?"

"It isn't really like that. I think about it all the time whether or not I want to, and writing a character that deals with what I go through every day of my life has been cathartic, to be honest."

Then she asks me a question I haven't thought of. "If the character uses sex to control her urges to do heroin, are you writing about yourself? Do you do that?"

"Yes and no. I have an addictive personality, so I can get addicted to anything. What I usually turn to when I want heroin is alcohol, but I'm not going to lie. I'm already addicted in some way to how it feels when you and I are together. I tell myself that I should keep my hands off you, like when you got here tonight, but then you kissed me and all I could think about was how much I wanted to be inside you."

All this confessing makes me feel exposed and more vulnerable than I like, so I get up to find myself some scotch to make the uneasiness go away. Kristina follows me and as I pour myself a drink, she wraps her arms around me like she did earlier in the kitchen and whispers against my back, "I know what you mean. I have a hard time being around you without touching you. I've never felt like this. I thought it was just me who had this weakness."

I swallow a gulp of the scotch, enjoying the warmth it spreads as it goes down my throat, and turn to face her. "I'm not sure what it is, but I don't want you to think I'm using you for sex because I'd rather be high. That's not it at all."

She gives me one of her sweet smiles and looks up at me with such caring in her eyes I want to believe she won't run.

"Your weaknesses don't frighten me off, Ian. I see in your face you're worried they do. They don't, though. As long as mine don't frighten you off."

I tuck her hair behind her left ear and trace my finger along her jaw. "That addiction to people your therapist claims you have? I can think of much worse things than having you addicted to me."

"I want you to know how much I think of you telling me all this tonight. I know you didn't have to confide in me like this. It means a lot to me."

There's no way I can avoid telling her the absolute truth now, so I kiss her and take her hand as we walk back to the couch. I don't let go of her hand as I say the words I know might make what she just said a lie. "I don't ever want to go back to where I was, but that doesn't mean it won't happen. I've never gone this long without it, but as much as I want to promise you I won't let it back into my life, it's something that haunts me every day and night."

"Will you promise me something?"

"Yes," I answer, happy to see the kindness in her eyes hasn't left yet.

"Promise me if you ever do want to go back that you'll tell me because I can't stand by and watch someone I care about ruin his life. I know what I'm supposed to say is that I'd be by your side and help you through it, but I can't promise that like you can't promise it won't ever happen again. I'm not strong enough."

"You'd leave if I went back to it?"

"I'm sorry, but yes, I would. That's not what people want to hear, but it's the truth, and I promise I will always tell you the truth. I can't watch you kill yourself. I care too much about you already to do that, and there's no way you'll want me more than some drug. I wish that wasn't the case, but I've been around enough people who do drugs in my business to know I'm no comparison. You'll choose the drug over me, if you have to make the choice."

I'm struck by her words. "I've never had anyone tell me they'd leave if I went back to using heroin. All they ever say is that they'll help me through it. Then I go back to it and they try to help, but you're right. I always choose the drugs over them. I don't want to do that this time, though."

Kristina rests her head on my chest and squeezes me to her. "I know, but if you do, you deserve to know what I'll do."

I stroke her soft hair and press a small kiss to the top of her head. "Thank you for being honest. Nobody's ever been honest like that with me before."

We talk for hours about the book and how I hope the story will turn out, but Kristina's promise to me that if I choose the drugs over her that I'll lose her never leaves my mind. That woman I saw on my television is far stronger than I ever could be. As we lay naked in each other's arms later, I already know there's no way I could give her up, no matter what.

Unlike my character, the sex isn't what I'm addicted to. I'm addicted to her, and she's as much a drug as anything I've ever snorted up my nose.

CHAPTER SEVEN

Kristina

I SIT IN Ian's living room as I have every night for the past week listening to him read me what he's written in our story that day. That's how I think of Silk. Our story. I know he's the one writing it and it's his talent that will make it a success, but when I hear his words on the page that are there because I'm his muse, I can believe it's our story.

He takes on a whole new look when he's writing, a look that enchants me even more than the one he had when we met. His features intensify, as if telling our story brings out all the emotion in him. I watch his face as he reads me the day's words and see the fire in his eyes when he reaches a part he's written from a memory of our being together. Those dark eyes become pools reflecting his desire just like when he makes love to me.

"I wrote a scene today I'm not sure I'll keep in

the final draft."

"Is that how this works? I guess I just always thought you wrote the book from start to finish," I say as I take a drink of wine.

"I do write that way, essentially, but my muse is inspiring me to write things that I usually wouldn't."

Smiling, I lean in and kiss him on the cheek. "Your muse?"

He winks and gives me a crooked smile. "Yes, my muse. Would you like to hear more?"

"Always. I want to hear everything, and then when the book comes out, I'll buy dozens of copies and tell everyone I was the inspiration for it."

Ian's face suddenly morphs to a far more serious look. "No, Kristina. You can't tell anyone. Remember, you promised?"

The gorgeous desire in his eyes vanishes, leaving only the darkness that makes me feel like he's disappointed in me. Quickly, I take his hand in mine. "I know. I was just saying I'd be proud. Don't worry. I won't do anything."

"As long as you understand that telling anyone would mean ruin for me. I can't let the world know about this."

I cling to him, afraid he's angry with me. "I won't. I promise. I would never do anything to hurt you or your career, Ian. I know how important the public's perception is. As much as I want to tell everyone about you and me and this book, I won't. You can trust me."

I wait for him to answer, my heart pounding in my chest as I silently chastise myself for being so stupid. The man tells me I can't tell the world about us or his new book, and what do I say? That the first thing I'll do when it's released is tell everyone about us.

A slow smile spreads across his lips, and he kisses me on the forehead. "It's okay. I'm excited too. And I know you understand why we have to keep this quiet. I'm happy you want to share this with the world. I wish we could."

"We get to share it with each other. That's even better."

An awkward silence settles in between us as he goes back to silently reading over what he wrote. After a few minutes, he looks up and says, "Ready for more?"

Nodding, I snuggle up next to him and listen as he tells me more of Kate Silk's story.

"I reach the top of the stairs and feel him behind me. His warm breath skims my shoulder as he leans in to put his key in the lock, and the hardness of his cock grazes my ass just light enough to make me want more. I look around to see the hallway empty and turn to face him. 'Feeling brave, Jake?' He says nothing, but I see in his eyes he knows what I want and wants it too."

Ian looks up from the paper and smiles. "What do you think?"

"That's not from anything you and I have done before. Fantasy? Or is this something you've done with someone else?"

A rush of jealousy takes me over at the thought of Ian with another woman. It's irrational, I know, but I don't want to think of him with anyone else. Just me.

"No one else. I just took what we did in the kitchen the other night and moved it to the hallway," he explains, much to my relief.

"Oh. I thought maybe..." I don't finish my sentence because it will just sound insecure and stupid.

Putting the paper down on the coffee table, he stares at me as if he knows what I was going to say. "Come here," he says as he pulls me onto his lap. "You don't think I could be with someone else other than you, do you?"

I'm not sure how to answer his question. Of course I think that. I've never been with a man who didn't cheat on me. "I don't know. This has all happened so fast."

He slides his hands down my back to cup my

ass and pulls me into him. Pressing his lips to my ear, he says in a voice that makes me pool with wetness, "There is no one but you. Whether in real life or in the book, it's all you, Kristina."

Closing my eyes, I relish his words. *It's all you, Kristina.* I love the sound of his voice as he says them. It makes each syllable all the more special. It makes me feel special.

I lean back and smile at him staring up at me like he means what he says. "Will you read me anymore before I have to go?"

He shakes his head. "No, I'll save it for next time. Why do you have to leave so soon?"

My mouth opens to speak, but I'm distracted by his finger slowly sliding down over my damp panties. "I have to...I mean I have an appointment...Ian, I can't think when you touch me like that."

His gaze is fixed on my panties as he says, "I love it when your voice whines like that. It's cute."

My eyes roll back into my head when he slips the tip of his finger under the cotton and touches my clit, sending zings of need straight to my core. "And when you touch me like this, I can't think of anything but fucking. I can't do that, though, because I have to go to my meeting and I can't go smelling like sex."

"It's not sex," he whispers as he softly rubs the pad of his thumb in circles over my needy clit.

"If I come, it's sex."

His dark eyes flash up at me. "Then I won't let you come."

I knit my brows at the thought of him touching me like this and not letting me come. "Why would you want to torture me?"

Moving his hand lower, he slides his middle finger inside me. "You were the one who said you can't go to your meeting smelling like sex."

I begin to rock against his palm, but he stops me. Confused, I lean down to kiss him and whisper against his lips, "Please, Ian. Don't tease me."

"I'm not teasing," he says while he slides a second finger into my wet pussy. "No coming for you, Kristina."

"Then I'll just have to do it myself when I get home," I say with a pout.

"I thought I told you not to do that," he scolds, roughly pulling his fingers out of me.

I don't know what to say. He seems like he's being playful, but something in his expression— an edge that isn't normally there—makes me think he's angry with me. I still want to get off and feel a little angry that he's playing with me.

"Fine. I'll just go to my meeting now and go

home to do nothing. Let me up."

Half-expecting him to refuse to release me, I'm surprised when he swings his hands out to the side giving me free passage to get off his lap. Straightening my skirt, I grab my purse and head for the door, hurt and confused by his behavior, but if I stay I'm liable to say something hurtful that I don't mean and ruin everything.

As my hand touches the doorknob, I feel him come up behind me. I don't turn around, part afraid of what I'll say and part hurt that he'd play with me like this. His arm slips around my waist, instantly making my resolve weaken.

In my ear, he says low and deep, "Don't leave."

Staring forward at the door, I close my eyes and steel myself. I don't want to give in. I don't. But he has this effect on me. "I have to go."

"I know. Don't."

Slowly, I turn around to see him looking at me with such need in his eyes. I don't understand his behavior. "Ian, I don't like to be toyed with."

He leans down and kisses me like he's never kissed me before—deeper, longer, and more intense than anyone has ever kissed me. When I think I can't go on for another second longer, he pulls away and cradles my face. Looking deep into my eyes, he says in a voice that nearly breaks my heart, "Forgive me. That wasn't fair of me to test you like that."

"Test me? Why would you feel like you need to test me?" I ask as he presses his forehead to mine.

"I don't know. It's stupid and I'm sorry, Kristina. I just felt like you didn't care."

I look into those dark eyes and see he's truly worried I don't care about him. But how could he think that? Every night I come here to be with him. To listen to his deep voice speak those beautiful words he's written because of me. How could I not care?

"I care more than I should after just a few days of knowing you, Ian. We've been like a flood of emotions that's carried me away since the moment we met. I can't think of anything else but you when we're not together, and when we are, all I can think about is how much I want to feel your hands on my body. If I made you think I don't care, I'm sorry."

He shakes his head and frowns, making me feel worse. "No, you did nothing wrong. This is all my fault. Forgive me."

"How about I come back after my meeting and show you how much I care? I shouldn't be too long."

Another kiss that makes my legs feel like

they're jelly and he leans back away from me with a smile. "I'll be here."

"Okay. I'll be back."

CAFÉ EUROPA IS crowded, like usual. Every table is full, and people even stand along the walls, obscuring the beautiful blue and grey mosaic design of what I imagine is supposed to be the Mediterranean. My friend Priscilla sits at a table in the back of our favorite café looking as gorgeous as ever. Her newest style includes a short cut for her blond hair and lots of brown for her smoky eye look. I don't know how she does it, but she pulls off wearing all that makeup in the middle of the day. I'd look like a hooker if I did it.

"Kristina! I was early, so I ordered us those delicious croissant sandwiches we love. Sit down and tell me what you've been up to lately. You look practically glowing. You're not pregnant, are you?"

The patrons at the tables around us turn to look at me after Priscilla's announcement, and I smile meekly hoping they will just return to their conversations and ignore me.

"Can you keep your voice down?" I whisper as I sit down. "Everyone doesn't need to know my business."

She rolls her eyes like I've said something ridiculous. "You know, for a celebrity, you're pretty shy about things. This is the age of TMZ, baby. Everybody wants to know everything."

"There's nothing to know. Everything there is to know is up on the screen, like it should be. What I do in my private time is just that. Private."

"Well, share what skincare regimen you're using because you look fantastic. Your skin has a glow to it that I've only seen in pregnant women."

"Well, I'm not pregnant, so you can stop saying that."

"Then I have to know what you're using because I want a case of it. My skin is starting to look like crepe paper."

I stare at her in disbelief. Priscilla is one of the most beautiful women in the world, and she has the men lining up around the block to prove it. Her skin looks as stunning and dew-kissed as it always has. Ten thousand dollar spa treatments do that for a woman.

"Can we talk about something that has some basis in reality?"

Arching one perfectly manicured eyebrow, she sneers at me. "You make fun, but this face is on its last leg. I'm going to need a full facelift before I'm thirty at this rate."

Thankfully, the waiter interrupts our ridiculous conversation with our tuna croissant sandwiches. Priscilla hadn't been wrong about them. They're delicious and the only reason I agreed to come here to spend time with her in such a public place.

Even their scrumptiousness doesn't stop Priscilla's need to talk, though, and it doesn't take long for her to get back to pumping me for information on why I look so happy. I want to tell her all about Ian. Smarter than most of my boyfriends, he's someone I'm proud to be with. The problem is that she has a big mouth, and she'll tell the entire world about us before the afternoon is up.

So I lie. Sort of.

"I've begun a cleanse I heard about from one of the makeup artists on my last film, so maybe that's why my skin is doing the glowing thing. I've also been seeing someone, but I think my giving up drinking hard liquor might also be helping me look better. You know what they say. Alcohol saps the youth right out of your face. Or is that smoking? I'm not sure."

Priscilla narrows her eyes to suspicious slits and leans forward, pointing her index finger toward me. "What was that middle part? Did you say you're seeing someone new?"

"Yes, but my guess is the lack of booze is what's making my skin glow. You should try it."

She raises her eyebrows as if I've just said something utterly ridiculous. "I'm never giving up alcohol, thank you, but stop trying to get off the topic. Who is he? I want all the deets!"

Taking the last bite of my sandwich, I make sure to chew far slower than I usually would to stem the tide of madness I know will come as soon as I begin speaking again. When I'm finally finished, I take a drink of my iced tea and smile, knowing Priscilla is about to go out of her mind with curiosity. I can't tell her much, but I will take a few moments to brag about Ian, albeit anonymously.

"He's just someone I met because of one of my movies."

"What the hell does that mean? Met because of one of my movies could mean some guy who asked you for your autograph on the street. I want real info, Kristina."

I see I'm not going to get out of this without some details, so I go with the obvious. She'll draw her own wrong conclusions, if I'm lucky. "He's a writer, okay? There. That's all I'm going to say about him other than he's a great guy and I'm having a great time with him."

"Oooooh, I love it! You haven't had a real

romance since John, so it's about time."

Priscilla's mention of John makes my heart contract for a moment, but I make sure to smile so she doesn't see the effect on me from hearing his name. I don't love him anymore, but his leaving me for some waitress at a hotel bar in San Francisco still stings.

"It's not a big deal," I lie, hoping she'll drop this topic of conversation and return to her concern for her impending facelift.

"If you say so, but your face says something else. Whatever he's doing for you, keep it up. And when you're done with him, send that man my way so I can get whatever he's got for my face."

Quickly, I seize the opportunity to bring up the facelift again. "Are you really thinking of getting some work done, Cilla? I don't think you need it at twenty-six."

With her fingertips, she pushes the skin up from her jawline until she looks like she's shoving her head through a hole too small for it. "Gravity is such a bitch, Kristina. She's a bitch, I tell you. How will I ever get a man with these jowls?"

"You don't have jowls. You have a jaw that wishes you'd stop abusing it like that. As for getting a man, you never have a problem in that department. Just because you haven't dated anyone you like in months isn't a reason to go searching for a bridge to jump from, or in your case, a plastic surgeon to carve into you."

Cilla lifts her right hand up and pledges, "I'm deciding here and now to wait for you to be done with your mystery man writer so then I can look fantastic. Until then, it's the spa for me. I'm going after this. Want to come? Alexander's would be happy to have a star with them, even though you don't have an appointment. They're such celebrity whores."

"I can't. I have to meet with my agent. You know how Jennie gets. If I miss a meeting, she's sure I've run away to another agent behind her back."

I don't entirely lie, but my meeting with my agent isn't until the next day. I just don't want to get trapped in a seaweed wrap with Priscilla pumping me for information about Ian. I might not be able to stop myself from telling her something, and then I know it will only be a matter of hours before the paparazzi hunt us down like rabid dogs and ruin everything between Ian and me.

"Time for me to head out. When are you leaving for LA?" I ask as I stand to leave.

Priscilla looks up at me and smiles at my mention of LA. She hates New York as much as I love it, so I know she's eager to return to the sun of southern California. "Saturday. Marlie is having her annual Octoberfest party. I'm hoping it's not half-naked men in lederhosen again. I mean, they were hot, but lederhosen? What the fuck?"

"I'm glad I missed it. Men in lederhosen, no matter how hot, is not what I want to see," I say with a chuckle.

"I'll be back in town by Christmas, I think. Promise me we'll get together then, and I'm going to expect more details about this mystery man."

Leaning down, I hug her goodbye and promise I'll meet up with her for the holidays. Maybe by then I can tell her more about Ian too.

As I leave the café, a man standing on the sidewalk just outside the door asks for my autograph and I politely sign a sheet of paper for him, hoping to avoid any photographers wanting to snap pictures of me this afternoon. Cilla may think I'm glowing, but that doesn't mean I want to be anything but a normal person just out for a bite to eat with a friend.

The fan smiles and thanks me, but from behind him a man lurches toward me and grabs my arm. Slightly taller than the first man, he's about my height and has a mousey look to him with a pointy nose and chin that reminds me of a rat. I recoil from his touch, but his fingers close in around my sweater.

"Kristina, I've waited so long to meet you!" he exclaims as he pushes closer to me. "You're the most beautiful woman I've ever seen."

Terrified, I merely nod and turn to get away, but his hold on me keeps me planted in place. I don't know what to do and as my emotions quickly spin out of control, I remember the last time a fan did this and I fell apart for weeks afterward. I open my mouth to cry for help, but thankfully the first fan helps me and tugs the man off me, giving me the chance to run away as a crowd of people begin to form a tight circle around us.

I quickly force my way through them and make my way to Ian's apartment instead of going home, checking over my shoulder for any cameras as I get out of the cab, but thankfully, I seem to have eluded them today. My legs haven't stopped shaking since that fan grabbed me, and I feel weak. In truth, with all the celebrity scandals from secret babies to repeated stints in drug rehabs, I'm relatively boring and not really fodder for the front pages of gossip magazines anymore.

Not that I miss that. But fans are a different story. They don't need drama to want to be next to me.

Ian answers his door wearing that smile I

already love. Taking me in his arms, he nuzzles my neck. "How was your meeting?"

"Unproductive," I say, still shaking. "How was your afternoon?"

"Why are you shaking? What happened, Kristina?"

Closing the door, he escorts me to the living room, his hand on my lower back as always to guide me. I sit down and try to take in a full breath. "It wasn't a big deal. A fan just grabbed me and I got scared."

Ian holds my face in his hands and looks at me like all he sees is a broken bird. "Are you okay?"

"I am now. Tell me about your afternoon so I can forget that awful, rat-faced man who grabbed me.

"I wrote a little more and had lunch. Such is the exciting life of an author," he says as he holds me so my head rests on his chest.

I look up at him and ask, "Can I have a glass of that wine I brought over? It's one of those chilly October days and it would hit the spot right now."

He kisses me and stands up from the couch. "Sit down and relax. I'll get it."

I love how he dotes on me like this. Most men I've known would have sat down on the couch and pointed toward the kitchen, saying, "Sure. Grab me a glass too while you're at it."

But not Ian.

"Here you go," he says as he hands me the wine glass. "You're going to need more of that, so I'll pick it up when I go out later."

Most men wouldn't do that either.

"You're so sweet," I coo and he beams his happiness at my compliment.

"Not all sweet."

He turns to face me and kisses me hard, like he's missed me for the few hours I've been gone. Need coils in my abdomen as he snakes his tongue into my mouth and his hands close into fists in my hair, tugging it not so gently.

"I missed you," he says and then teases my lips with his tongue. "You taste good."

"I had tuna fish for lunch," I admit, my cheeks warming from a blush of embarrassment. "I wanted the wine because I was worried I had bad breath."

Ian shakes his head and kisses me again hard and full on the lips. "Nope. But it wouldn't matter if you did. I'd still want you more than my next breath at this moment."

His hand leaves my hair and travels down to slide up underneath my skirt. Grazing my panties, he slides his finger along the edge, sending chills up my spine. I can't help but want him as much as I did a few hours before when things went wrong.

His words…his touch…I'm his for the taking.

I clumsily try to unzip his pants, wishing for once he sat around his house naked so I could just sit on his lap and feel him slide inside me. Pushing my hand away, he finishes the job and pulls his boxer briefs down to reveal his cock hard and ready for me. I hike my skirt up around my waist, forgetting I wore underwear because I was meeting Cilla.

Looking down, I smile. "I usually don't wear those when I know I'm coming here."

Ian's gaze travels to my panties. I move to stand so I can take them off, but in a flash he rips them off me and tosses them to the side. "Problem solved. Now get back here so I can bury my cock in your tight cunt."

He pulls me down hard onto him, filling me quickly until he's fully nested and stretching me to take all of him. His cock touches a spot inside me that sends strings of pleasure through my body, but when he lifts me off him to plunge back into me, I want to cry out in ecstasy.

"You like that?" he asks in a sexy voice.

"Yes," I say more as a moan than anything else as I begin to ride him.

"That's it, baby. Ride my cock. Let me see you come apart on top of me."

His fingers dig into my hips as he decides how fast I should go. I roll my hips so his cock slides over my G-spot and watch the look on his face as he sees how much I love the feel of him. He's power and desire, and I can't get enough of him.

I want to feel his touch on the rest of my body, so as I ride him, I strip off my sweater and bra. He senses what I need without a word spoken between us and cups my breasts in his hands, squeezing my nipples hard between his thumbs and fingers just the way he already knows I like it.

"Ohhhh….Ian," I moan. I'm close already. I just need him to stay right where he is and I'll come.

Then he touches my clit and as I close my eyes, everything looks like colors exploding in the darkness. My body surrenders to his, and I come harder than I thought I could, bucking wildly on him as he holds me down on his cock. The feeling is more incredible than anything I've ever felt in my life. Clinging to him as wave after wave of sensation fills me, I finally collapse against him, unsure even if I can hold myself up anymore.

"Oh, my God. That was mind blowing," I whisper in his ear. "But you didn't come yet."

"Not yet. I was thinking your mouth could do

the job."

Leaning back, I feel his cock twitch inside me. "You do like that, don't you?"

He gives me a devilish smile. "You sucking my cock after I've made you come? Yeah. I think it's sexy that you can taste yourself on me as you suck me off."

"Then your wish is my command," I say as I ease myself off his lap to kneel in front of him. Taking his cock into my mouth, I taste myself on his skin. "Anything else you find sexy while I'm down here?" I joke.

"Yeah, but all in due time. For now, just watching you suck me off will be all I need."

I slowly take all of him into my mouth, tasting myself on his silky skin as each delicious inch of his cock slides over my lips. Staring up at him as ecstasy fills his expression, I push the uneasiness I still feel about my abilities out of my mind and enjoy the feeling of pure sensuality giving him pleasure gives me.

Never before have I felt so sexy, and I love it. And even though I know it might not be the best way to handle things, having sex with Ian helps take my mind off that awful fan and how frightened he made me.

CHAPTER EIGHT

Ian

I WAKE UP alone and instantly miss Kristina's gentle touch against me first thing in the morning. The bed feels too big for one person now since she's been in it. Stretching my arm out to the side, I run my hand over the cool sheets where she would be. I bury my face in the pillow next to me and smell the faint scent of her perfume, soft and flowery.

Two weeks. That's all it's been and already I can't stand to be away from her for more than a few hours. My limbs ache from want as my mind replays our time together last night. The feel of her tight cunt gripping me like a glove as she rode me so wildly. The taste of wine on her lips when she kissed me just as she came so hard I thought she'd strangle my cock. The sound of her voice when she told me how much she'd miss me when she was leaving.

I know I should slow things down between us.

The warning signs are all there. She's tender and sweet, and when she finds out the monster addiction makes me, she'll run away. I won't be able to let her, but she'll want to. She'll say it's too much—too fast—too overwhelming. I'll tell her I can't live without her and mean every syllable.

What I don't know is how she'll react after that. The problem is that I do know how I will react. As much as heroin or alcohol, I'm addicted to her, and just like with them, she controls every moment of my day.

And I can't imagine a day without her.

I take a deep breath and hold the air in my lungs until I can't hold it anymore, letting it out slowly until there's nothing left to release. I feel the tiny bit of control I still possess begin to slip away.

SHEILA'S OFFICE REMINDS me of what I imagine a study in a college professor's house would look like. The predominant color is brown. Dark walnut wood bookcases line the walls to each side of her desk, which is also dark walnut. The three leather chairs, including the one she sits in, are a caramel brown with black metal studs that look brown.

The room has a warm feel I've never found

anywhere else in the world, no matter how many beautiful homes I've been in. That's pure Sheila, though. Warm. Comforting. Nurturing.

She's summoned me to her office to talk about my next book, which in fact doesn't even exist as the kernel of an idea yet. I haven't decided what I'm going to tell her when she gets around to asking about it. Right now, she's going on about the dozens of calls she's been fielding for another of her authors who committed the cardinal sin of sounding off on social media about some reviewer or something. This is why I pay people to be me online. I don't have the time for that bullshit.

"So I've been putting out fires for the last twenty-four hours, and Ian, you have no idea how big this might have gotten if I hadn't reeled her in," Sheila says frantically, her eyes darting left and right over the edge of her desk as she looks for something.

"You know how it is with the new ones," I say in my most comforting voice as I pretend to care. "And it's ten times as hard nowadays with everything you say being scrutinized. Better to say nothing at all, but then you're not social enough. It's a Catch-22. She'll find her way."

"A hundred times harder than when you got into this business a decade ago. Thankfully, I don't have those issues with you. You're smart enough to delegate your social media presence to those two girls, who I must say do a wonderful job. Maybe I should find a couple like them for Eva."

I'm not listening closely, but just to be polite I mumble, "Sounds good."

What I'm thinking about is how long this is going to take and when I'm going to see Kristina again. Just five more hours.

"So, we need to talk about your next book. The publisher isn't going to wait forever, Ian. They're dying to know what's next. Nero's Nightmare was a huge success, so capitalizing on that is key. What do you think you might want to do?"

I have a brand new three book deal that I have to honor, based on the early sales of Nero's Nightmare. Within the past three months, I've thought of exactly zero ideas for the next book. I know Sheila understands, but the reality is that writing isn't something like factory work. You don't just churn out ideas every day. At least not good ones. Good ideas take time. Great ideas take even longer.

But the publisher doesn't give a fuck about good or great ideas. They want books that will make money. Not that I'm against money, mind you. I'm a capitalist, so money is fine with me. But their wanting more money doesn't coincide with my ideas coming any faster.

However, if I don't tell Sheila something and make her think I'm working on the third book, she'll worry and then I won't have a moment's peace until I give her an idea.

So I lie.

"I'm thinking something with Marc Antony."

There. That should make her happy.

But it doesn't. Not really. I watch her unattractive face twist into an unsatisfied grimace. "Marc Antony? Are you sure?"

"Is there something wrong with Marc Antony? I'm not tied to the emperor idea as I was with the last two books. This is an entirely new series. When you pitched them the idea for this one, you told them it would be ancient Rome as the setting. So what's wrong with Antony?"

"He's just been done a lot in the past. What about that Pontius Pilate book you once mentioned to me? Now that would be a bestseller for sure."

Her enthusiasm for my jumping into some ugly religious fray makes me smile. "I did have some ideas for that, but that was years ago."

Sheila leans forward, a clear sign she wants to encourage this whole Pontius Pilate thing. "Why not explore it? An historical fiction book involving Pontius Pilate would be a hit!"

"I wrote the last two from a crime and political scandal perspective, Sheila. That wouldn't work for this, although I have to admit I'm no Pontius Pilate scholar."

I'm not trying to be self-effacing or humble. I truly only know marginally more than the average human being does about this historical figure. When I first mentioned it to her, I think I had just gotten out of rehab for the first time and was ingesting a healthy dose of religion to keep myself from going back to my old ways. Normally, I'm not really a religious person at all. Spiritual at times, but not religious.

"Well, think about it. I'll mention it and feel them out about it to see if it works for them."

That statement right there bothers me. Crossing my arms, I say, "How about an author writing what works for them? Does it always have to be what the publishers want?"

She sits back in her chair and sighs. No doubt, I'm becoming more difficult, like her young author who can't keep her mouth shut on Twitter. I don't care. Something about being a pawn who's supposed to write whatever the powers that be deem interesting has gnawed at me for a long time, and now that I'm secretly writing something on the side, their demands chafe me more.

"You know I'm a champion of artistic integrity, Ian. You know that. You also know that money is what makes this industry go 'round. If your books don't sell, I won't be able to get you those advances you like. I would never let them tell you what to write, but understand my job here. I need to make you as marketable as possible."

I wonder aloud in frustration, "What happens to all those people who have great ideas that the publishers don't like?"

"They self-publish. It's all the rage. I'm not sure anyone writing historical fiction is terribly successful yet, but some are doing fantastic numbers. I know agents who are representing these authors and their numbers are impressive."

"Are we talking paying to print a book and getting stuck with boxes and boxes of them in someone's garage?"

Sheila smiles and her awkward appearance softens. "No. I'm talking about ebooks. You know, the Kindle and Nook. Millions of people around the world read books like that these days."

"Not until they come with the ability to produce that book smell I love."

"Well, you're old fashioned, Ian, but many

people love them."

Suddenly, an idea comes to me. "You say there are people selling their own books without publishers? What genres?"

"Romance and science fiction, mostly, I think. The Kindle basically exploded because of erotica and romance, and they've led the way. Those readers buy ebooks by a much greater margin."

"Hmmm…interesting." Now the wheels in my head are really turning.

"Oh, my God! Ian, you aren't thinking about that for your books, are you?" Sheila asks in that panicked voice she used just a few minutes ago when she was talking about that other author. "Please tell me you're not."

Shaking my head, I work to put her mind at ease before that vein in her forehead explodes out from under the skin. "No. Don't worry. I was just thinking that's going to be something that will make publishers have to change and maybe authors will be able to write more of the books they want."

Sheila exhales and hangs her head for a moment before she looks up at me with a look of pure relief on her face. "Thank God. You gave me a scare for a minute there. Can we get back to the reality of your next book with a publisher? Can I tell them about Pontius Pilate?"

"Tell them I'm mulling over ideas and deciding between Marc Antony and Pontius Pilate."

"Okay, okay. I just don't want to see you become complacent, Ian. You have real talent. After all you've been through, I'd hate to see you let it all go because you lost your passion."

I stand and give her a wink. "Not to worry, Sheila. I haven't lost my passion. Trust me."

"Good. And I hope you don't mind me saying that you look great. I was worried after our last phone call, but I'm glad to see you're looking healthy and happy."

"Thanks, Sheila. Nobody worries about me like you."

As I head toward the door, she yells after me, "I'll call you when I hear something. And don't forget about the film deal. It's almost done."

I wave goodbye and head out the door with my mind already moving on from what she wants me to think about to what I want to focus on.

Kristina.

✧　✧　✧

I HOP IN a cab to head back home and as we get stuck in midday traffic, I think about Sheila's comments about self-publishing. Could it work for Silk? A bigger concern is using my name on the book. As an author of historical fiction, I likely don't have many fans who also read erotic books. Talk about an interesting Venn diagram for that group.

No, I'm going to need a pseudonym. I have no idea what I might want to call myself. Should it be something clever or sexy like names in porn? Maybe something like Ian Cox? Or Ian Cumming? I chuckle as I say the names to myself. No, they won't work. Maybe something with an initial and some generic name.

The cab passes a bank truck with the name Anderson written on the driver's side door. Nice common name. Now for an initial. My mind quickly moves to memories of watching Wheel of Fortune in my freshman dorm room at college with my roommate who was so obsessed with Vanna White he could barely get through a whole show without heading to the bathroom to jerk off. The most common letters are given in that final round—R, S, T, L, N, and E. I go through each letter, disliking the sound of most of them, but T doesn't sound bad.

T. Anderson. I like the double entendre of T and A in the name of an erotica author. Chuckling to myself, I decide that name will work. Silk by T. Anderson.

I finally reach my building and jump out of

the cab, happy I've got a name and a possible means of publishing the book. The sun has finally found a way to peek out from behind the clouds that have obscured it all day, so I choose to go for a walk instead of shutting myself up inside. It doesn't take long for me to know where I'm headed.

Ten minutes later, I'm standing across the street from Kristina's building staring up at her second floor windows into her living room. I think about that first night together in that room and how she'd been so afraid I didn't like her because of what happened with some asshole. I still had no idea who he was. It hadn't occurred to me to bother to find out.

He was the past, and in this case for me, I didn't give a fuck about the past.

As I stare up at that room that holds such sweet memories for me, I wonder if she's home. My mind weaves a scene of her sitting on her leather sofa, her beautiful legs curled up under her as she reads a script. Or a book. One of mine. Her soft brown hair falls over her shoulders, teasing the tops of her full breasts so sensitive to my touch. Those cornflower blue eyes I fell in love with as I watched her films intently read the book in her lap, her perfectly shaped pink lips occasionally moving to mouth a word as the story comes alive for her.

I crave that mouth. I crave every part of her. In just a few short weeks, I've become a slave to my need for her. Addicted. Obsessed.

Lost.

CHAPTER NINE

Kristina

I ARRIVE AT Ian's apartment to find him deep in work on our book, his dark eyes flashing with inspiration as his fingers fly across the keyboard. I love watching him create like this.

After a few minutes, he sits back and smiles at me. "Just finished another chapter. I love how it's coming. Take a look."

He opens his arms for me, and I sit on his lap to read what he's written, sure it's as wonderful as everything else he's written. Before I can read a word, Ian pulls my face to his and kisses me long and deep. My body yearns for his touch, yearns for him to make love to me right now.

"I missed you," he whispers in a hoarse voice that hits me deep inside. "I've missed feeling of you next to me."

"I missed you too," I say as I slide my fingers through his dark hair. "I thought about you today. I was reading the inscription you wrote in my copy of Caligula's Dream. Your best fan. I love that."

His hand slowly caresses the tops of my thighs, teasing me every so often when he sneaks a finger over the front of my panties already damp from my desire for him. I watch his tongue slowly glide over his lower lip as his gaze travels to where his hand comes to rest, and I'm desperate for him to ease the ache inside me.

"I love how wet you get just from my touch," he says and presses his fingertip to my clit, sending a jolt of need through my body.

"I want you, Ian. Please don't tease."

He removes his hand from under my skirt and kisses me softly on the lips. "After we read the scene I just wrote."

I can't help but pout at his insistence in reading instead of getting me off, but I try to be understanding, even as he quickly shifts from lover mode to author mode. He turns the laptop to face me and begins to read and it doesn't take long for a sense of uneasiness to creep in between us.

His eyes fix on the words that tell how Kate Silk stands on the street across from her lover's house thinking about how much she cares for him, but all I hear is the story of a woman stalking a man. After too many brushes with the media and paparazzi, I feel nothing but dread at the idea of someone watching me from the street below.

I thought Ian felt the same way, but as he continues to read I realize Kate is him. Has he stood across the street from my building and watched my apartment windows for any sign of me like his character does? I want to ask him, but I'm too afraid of the answer.

Ian's fingers stroke the insides of my thighs as he speaks, but all I want to do is run. With every word, I'm more convinced than ever that the scene he's written is one he's lived out before with me.

I need to get away from this place.

I need to get away from him.

"Ian, I'm not feeling well," I say suddenly, tearing him out of his work.

He looks confused, but his expression changes to concern and he asks, "Are you okay? Is something wrong?"

Those dark eyes look at me like I'm more important than anything else in his world, but I can't forget how I felt as he read to me just moments before. I need to get out there now before he realizes I don't like what he's done.

"My stomach is upset. I need to go home."

He says nothing but studies my face for a long moment. "Is something wrong, Kristina?"

The edge in his voice tells me he knows something's wrong. I need to leave. Standing, I look for where I dropped my purse on the way in. "Just don't feel well. I'll call you after I lie down for a bit."

I scramble toward the door, forgetting to even kiss him as I leave like I always do. He follows me and catches my arm as I reach for the door. "I don't even get a kiss goodbye?"

I don't want to face him now. He scares me. But slowly, I turn to see him standing behind me, a look of hurt in his eyes. For a moment, I regret my fear. He's been nothing but sweet and accepting of me. The problem is even as that regret makes me feel bad, the fear of being stalked makes me feel much worse.

"Of course. I'm sorry," I say before I lean in and kiss him as I have every time I left his apartment.

This time is different, though. I can't come back here.

He tenderly cradles my face and looks into my eyes as if he's searching for the answer to why I seem so different. His gaze unnerves me, and I say in a shaky voice, "I'm sure it's just a touch of the bug or something. I'll call you."

"You don't want me to call you a cab? I know you only live a few blocks away, but if you're sick, you don't want to walk all that way."

He knows I'm lying. I see it in his eyes. He knows and he can't figure out what's wrong.

"I think a little fresh air will be good for me."

"Do you want me to walk you home?"

"No. I'll call you later."

His hands slip from my face, and I turn toward the door. A quick twist of the doorknob and I pull the door open and leave as he calls after me to be careful. I don't look back, afraid of feeling bad if I see hurt in his eyes or terrified if I see he knows I don't plan to come back here ever again.

I frantically press the down arrow to get the elevator to come, hoping he doesn't decide to ignore what I said and walk me home. It feels like it takes forever for it to finally arrive, and I step in and sag against the metal walls as I press the button for the ground floor. I let out a deep sigh as if I've been holding my breath for too long and look down to see my hands shaking.

The elevator doors open and I bolt out into the lobby, nearly running over the doorman as he stands talking to a woman about the weather or something. I hear him wish me a good night just as I hit the doors to the outside, but I don't reply.

The October wind hits me as I step onto the sidewalk, making me all the more conscious of how much I want to be safe and sound in my home. I run down the block toward my building, turning around once or twice to see if Ian's behind me, but I don't see him. Maybe he believed my lie.

When I finally reach my apartment, I truly do feel sick to my stomach. The vision of him standing on the street watching my every move as I walk around my apartment blissfully ignorant of being stalked terrifies me.

But deep inside a tiny voice whispers that he would never hurt me. Ian cares for me. I'm his muse. He would never mean to frighten me intentionally.

I want to think all this is true, but then I remember him reading that scene so full of details of his character watching the one she loves and all I feel is afraid.

Afraid of him.

Closing my apartment door, I fasten every lock and deadbolt, something I never do when I'm home. I see his book sitting where I left it on my coffee table when I walk to my windows to draw the shades and a pang of loss bites at my heart. Curling up on the couch, I hold the book to my heart and sob. Had I been wrong to leave him? Was that voice that told me Ian would never hurt me right, or was my fear of him stalking me like a crazed fan right?

I pick up my phone to text him, but I don't know the words to say. Finally, my fingers type the only words that make sense.

I can't see you anymore.

Seconds later, his text comes in.

Why?

I just can't. I'm sorry.

He answers immediately with a text that breaks my heart. *I love you. Please don't leave me.*

As the tears roll down my face, I type *I'm sorry. We can't be together anymore.*

He doesn't answer, and my sadness grows until I want to call him and know why he won't speak to me anymore. I know it's crazy. I love him too, but I know my fear is real. How will I go on without him after everything we've been to one another?

My therapist is right. I am addicted to people. No, not people. Him. I'm addicted to him.

How will I be able to let him go?

As the reality of life without Ian settles into my brain, my phone vibrates against my leg one more time. Looking down, I see his reply to me.

There is no running from what we are, Kristina. I crave your touch as much you crave mine. There's no point in denying it. We will see each other again.

Terror courses through me as I read his words again and again. *We will see each other again.* I walk to the window to see if he's standing down on the sidewalk across the street watching me, waiting for me to open the blinds and see him. People walk past my building, but he's not there. I stand there for a long time peeking out to see if he ever shows up.

He doesn't.

In some small way, I wish he would. I know that's crazier than even I want to admit, but I'm disappointed when I finally step away from the window an hour later. I sit back down on the couch where he and I first kissed and made love and read over his message one more time.

There is no running from what we are, Kristina.

IAN AND KRISTINA'S STORY CONTINUES IN ADORE (ADDICTED TO YOU #2) GET YOUR COPY TODAY!

IF I DREAM
(CORRUPTED LOVE #1)

A story of passion, crime, and the lengths you go to for love…

If I dream, will you dare?

Ryder
All I wanted was my freedom. It's all I'd dreamed of from the first time I stood in the ring. Until I entered Robert Erickson's world. Until Serena. Cruelty and ugliness surrounded me, but she was beautiful and good. I wanted to protect her from her father's world, even though I knew being with her could mean the end of me.

Serena
I wanted for nothing as the daughter of one of the richest men in the world. But all my father's money couldn't buy what I truly craved. Until Ryder. I wanted all he was, all he brought out in me. All he made me desire.

Our love was forbidden by the one person who had the power to harm us. We dreamed of more than living in that world, though. We dreamed of having it all, but did we dare?

CHAPTER ONE

Ryder

A s usual, the crowd at The Pit screamed its lust for the two of us to pound the fuck out of each other. Impatient bastards. I couldn't hear any one person's words clearly, but I'd done this enough times to know what the people who'd come to watch us wanted.

Blood. Pain. And one of us as close to death as possible. It thrilled them in some sick way almost as much as I suspected winning did when their fighter crushed another person.

My opponent tonight stood nearly as tall as I did at six foot three, but his body was smaller than mine. He looked older, like something in the way he carried himself said he'd seen more of life than I had. His angular face looked hard, and on either side of his perfectly straight nose were eyes staring me down like he thought squinting and grimacing would make me run for the nearest exit like some fucking scared little boy. He was fighting the wrong person if that's what he expected.

I'd never lost and for good reason. When you had nothing but the feel of your fists beating the hell out of someone and the sound of those rabid fucks cheering you on like you were some kind of hero for nearly killing another man, all you wanted was to win.

Fifteen times I'd won right here in this dank warehouse against guys bigger and stronger than me, and every time it seemed to surprise everyone. Even those who had bet on me.

If they only knew how unlikely it was anyone could match the rage inside me, they'd never bet against me again.

Some impatient bastard behind me barked, "Stop dancing around! Hit 'em!"

Mr. Grimace narrowed his eyes until he could barely see out of them and took a deep breath. Why did he bother with all this tough guy bullshit? That's not what these bloodthirsty fucks wanted.

Pain is what they wanted.

So that's what they'd get. His or mine. It didn't matter to them.

"Scared, motherfucker?" he grunted out in a deep voice I knew wasn't really how he talked. "I'm going to fuck you up."

I didn't bother answering.

He caught me in the face with a hard right that scrambled my brains for a second, and then his fist skidded along my jaw and ran square into my right shoulder. The last guy I fought had done a number on that one, so that hurt like a bitch.

I knew how this went, though. The people around us wanted a show as much as they wanted a fight. I could have just beat the fuck out of him and won, but that's not what this was. I'd been told that enough times to understand even if I could pound the piss out of a guy, I had to at least make it look like a fight and not just some sad beat down.

So that's what I did. I took a few hits, sometimes more than a few, and let it look like there was some chance I wouldn't win. The other guy got to feel pretty big in the shorts and the crowd got to feel like this was really a match between two fighters.

It wasn't, though.

He paraded around like a peacock, preening to the crowd while I gritted my teeth and pushed my shoulder back into place. I took a deep breath and waited for the moment I'd show him who he was dealing with.

Flush with the love of the crowd, he turned back to face me. A few shots into me had made him think he had a chance.

I stepped forward as he lunged at me and leveled my fist against his jaw. His head ricocheted back, sending him reeling for a second or two, but I didn't let up. My right hand zeroed in on his face again, this time connecting with his cheekbone. I felt it crack against my knuckles bulging out of my fist and saw him stagger back away from me.

But he would get no mercy from me. That wasn't what I was here for.

"Get him!" the crowd screamed as the guy cowered, hanging his head to protect his busted face.

That wouldn't help him, though. Not with me. I knew what my role was. I knew why all these people had come here tonight, and it wasn't to see mercy. Mercy was for suckers. Fuck mercy.

They wanted blood and pain, and blood and pain is what they'd get.

I walked toward him as a feeling of complete calm came over me. All the noise of the crowd around us faded away until all I heard were the words I told myself every time I stood to fight.

It's you or him. Nothing more. Either you win or he does, but if you lose, you'll have nothing.

He looked up and I saw the pleading in his eyes. I'd seen it fifteen times before. No matter how big and tough they'd been in the beginning, each one ended up giving me that same sad look that said they wanted me to be someone other than who they'd heard I was.

Someone other than who I had to be.

Maybe they fought for some reason that had nothing to do with their very survival. Maybe they thought it would be fun, or it would make them feel tough. Maybe they thought they had something to prove to some girl. Whatever their reasons for agreeing to fight, they weren't why I fought.

For me, every win put me one step closer to being free. I didn't fight for shits and giggles or because I wanted to impress some skirt. I fought for the chance that one day I would never have to step foot in this fucking shithole place again. I fought because deep in the back of my mind there existed the tiniest dream that one day I'd be normal and have a normal life.

That one day I wouldn't have to be the man I'd been forced to become in this fight.

I knew his weak spots and attacked them. My fists pummeled his face, and no matter how hard he tried to shield himself from the blows, it was no use. Over and over, I hit him until that pretty face of his looked like mangled hamburger. Blood, flesh, and bone mixed to make a horror show. The nose that had been so straight just a few minutes before now pointed down toward his mouth like some deranged compass.

As I stood up to my full height, I heard the crowd cheering, as if I'd done something worthy of praise. A man lay in a crumpled heap at my feet, defeated and broken, and these fuckers were thrilled about it.

Looking around, I saw some clapping and others pumping their fists in the air as my win filled them with some kind of messed up happiness. Who was I kidding? What it filled was their wallets. That's why they were so happy.

Floyd raised my right arm in the air to the delight of the rabid fans and said in my ear, "That's my boy. You done good, son."

I forced a smile and nodded my head. I wasn't his boy and he wasn't my father. I was his fighter and he was the scumbag who went out to find people for me to fight. Whatever else he thought we were was all in his mind.

He lowered my arm and slapped me on the back. "Go relax. You deserve it. You put on a good show. Just look at the way these people love you!"

I tore my stare from his greasy comb-over and beady eyes and looked over his head to see the people who loved me. Between the booze, the drugs, and the fight, they looked like wild animals.

Who was worse? Them or me?

"RYDER, THERE'S SOMEONE here to talk to you,"
Floyd yelled from the other side of the door.

I didn't want to talk to anyone. All I wanted
to do was sit on my crappy metal folding chair in
this dingy room and hope my shoulder started
feeling better. I'd downed a few shots of Floyd's
whisky about ten minutes ago, but so far, it
hadn't helped ease the pain.

"Not now," I yelled back.

He'd only open the door anyway. I knew that.
It still felt good to let him and whoever the hell
was standing there with him know that I didn't
want to talk.

The door opened a second later and I saw
Floyd and some guy who looked far too well-
dressed to be anywhere near the warehouse on any
night standing in my shitty little room. He had a
vibe that screamed money with his suit, expensive
shoes, and slicked back grey hair that made him
look what my mother used to call stately.

"This is Mr. Robert Erickson," Floyd said as
the man walked into the room like he owned the
place. "I'll leave you two to talk."

I'd never seen Floyd leave a scene that fast. As
he closed the door, I looked at the man who stood

in front of me and saw he was studying me as much as I was him. Not that I was all too curious about what he wanted. People dressed like he was coming into my world never brought anything good with them.

Never.

The intruder looked around the cinder block room I called mine and then looked down at me. "Ryder, as our mutual friend Floyd said, my name is Robert Erickson. Do you know who I am?"

Shaking my head, I shrugged. "Nope. Should I?"

His dark eyebrows drew in like angry black slashes and his eyes narrowed to slits, much like the way the guy I just beat to a pulp had looked at the beginning of our fight. "I'm the man who runs this show. You are sitting in my warehouse and fighting in my stable. So yes, maybe you should know who I am."

As much as I knew he thought I should be impressed by this, I wasn't. Folding my arms across my chest, I said, "Oh yeah? Nice to meet the big boss then. I hope you bet on me tonight."

His eyes opened wider as the corners of his mouth inched up into what reminded me of how a crocodile looked right before he ate his prey. "You're pretty sure of yourself, aren't you?"

I looked up at the ceiling for a moment,

unsure how I should answer that. Fuck yeah, I was sure of myself. I may not have been wearing a thousand dollar suit and fine leather shoes like him, but I had gifts of my own that had made me a winner sixteen times already.

Pursing my lips, I shrugged again. "I haven't lost yet. Come see me when I do and I'll tell you how cocky I'm feeling then."

His crocodile smile spread even wider across his face. Nodding, he said, "I'll remember that. For now, I'm here to tell you I've bought your contract from Floyd. So now you work for only me."

The words hit me like a fist to the face. I didn't have a contract with Floyd or anyone else. I fought to pay off money I owed him, and when that debt was paid off, I'd get to leave this shithole world of fighting. Now all that seemed like a pipe dream this fucker had dashed to pieces.

I stood from my rusted metal chair and stared at Robert Erickson. "What does that mean?"

Nearly the same height, he met my gaze with one so intense I thought about taking a step back. When he spoke, it sounded like his voice came from somewhere dark.

"It means I own you now. You fight for me and I expect you to win like you always have."

Left unsaid was the implicit threat that hung

off every word. If you lose, you'll suffer. The only question was how.

My mind spun at the news that all I'd planned, all I'd worked for, was gone now. "So I guess my deal with Floyd to be released from fighting when I paid off what I owed him is gone too?"

"Yes."

"And if I don't agree to this new deal?" I asked, silently gauging my chances of not only getting past him but finding some way of surviving after I got away. He was big, and I had a sneaking suspicion even bigger guys stood outside waiting for him.

Robert Erickson looked like the type of man who got what he wanted, one way or another, whether the other person involved wanted it or not.

"You have no say in it, but let me assure you that you want to fight for me. For now, let's get you to your place so you can pack your things."

He turned to open the door as I explained this room was my place. "No need to go anywhere. You're already in it."

Erickson slowly looked back at me with confusion written all over his face. "You live here?"

I nodded. "Yeah. Short commute time to

work and everything I need within arm's reach. What more could a guy ask for?"

Closing the door, he turned to face me. "How old are you?"

"Eighteen."

"And you live here, in my warehouse where Floyd holds fights for me?" he asked as he looked around my room again, this time with a look of disgust like the fact made him sick.

"Yep. Better than the street or jail. I might not get three hots, but I got a cot and a shower."

My answer didn't make the sickened expression leave his face, but he nodded anyway. "Well, gather your things. It's time to go."

I opened my mouth to ask where, but he walked out and left me standing there in that room I'd lived in for the past three months. As I stuffed the few clothes I owned, deodorant, and my toothbrush into a duffel bag, I thought wherever I was going had to be better than this place.

WE PULLED UP to a massive black gate between two even bigger rows of hedges and stopped momentarily as the driver got the go ahead to drive onto the property. I couldn't help but stare out the window as we drove up the long driveway past some kind of fountain that looked like something the Greek gods might swim in and a bunch of smaller hedges than the ones out front that looked like the gardener had cut them all into bird shapes. Robert Erickson was even richer than I'd first thought. Only insanely wealthy people lived in places like this.

The car stopped in front of a house so big I couldn't see all of it as I looked out the car window. Erickson tapped me on the arm as I stared out at the mansion and said, "Welcome home."

Home? This couldn't be my home. Instantly, the thought of what I'd have to do to live in a place like this raced through my mind. Fighting in The Pit wasn't going to be enough to live in a house like the one I saw in front of me.

I opened the car door and stepped out onto a stone driveway as I gaped at the house, which was even more impressive without the tinting of the car window getting in my way. Huge white columns towered above us to the second story of the gold colored home, and a glass front door so enormous I'd never seen one so big stood behind them.

"Follow me," was all Erickson said as he led the way to those doors. I couldn't imagine what waited inside after an outside this incredible.

I did as he ordered and caught up to him as he

walked into an entryway so big the sound of our shoes hitting the white marble tile on the floor echoed off the matching marble tiled walls. He strode through like nothing around us was special toward the most spectacular curved wrought iron staircase I'd ever seen.

Not that I had seen many curved staircases with wrought iron in my life. I think I'd seen either a grand total of two times in a magazine some girl had in English class one time. I really didn't have much interest in reading architectural magazines, but she did and since I wanted to get in her pants, I sat next to her after school as she told me all about her dreams of having a huge house with a curved staircase and a wrought iron railing one day.

She would have loved Erickson's place. For me, it made me feel small, something very few people or things had achieved in a long time. Not small, actually. More like insignificant.

As my head swiveled left and right to look at the artwork on the walls, Robert said, "Come in here to my office. I want you to meet some people."

My hand clutched the handle of my duffel bag tightly in my palm. Meet some people? I didn't even look like they'd let me on the property to be the goddamned gardener who made hedges into animal shapes and now he wanted to introduce me to some people?

That feeling of insignificance morphed into one of pure discomfort. I didn't belong there, no matter how much he wanted to parade me through the place, and whoever he wanted me to meet would know that as sure as I did.

He led me into his office, a room even bigger than the entryway and as dark as that was light. This room had dark green walls the color of a pool table and a dark wood floor. Floor to ceiling bookcases held books with names I'd never heard of and sculptures I guessed cost more than my life was worth.

"Wait here. I'll be right back," he announced before leaving as I continued to look around in awe.

Seconds later, he came back with two females and ordered them into his office. Neither one looked like him, but something about the way they acted told me they weren't servants or people he'd just basically bought, like me.

They stopped dead at the sight of me standing there in my old gym pants and black t-shirt and the one I figured was older spun around to look at him in disgust.

"Who is this?"

"Girls, this is Ryder. He's going to be living

here, so treat him like family."

Robert's proclamation infuriated her, and she shook her head angrily. "What, like a brother? You go out one night and get us a brother? Is that how it goes, Dad?"

He ignored her outburst and turned his two daughters to face me. "Ryder, the one who can't stop talking is Janelle. The other one is Serena."

"Hi," I mumbled, unsure if I should say anything.

They both stood staring at me like I was some foreign thing that needed to be removed and fast. The one named Janelle had short dark brown hair, and although I couldn't be sure since her eyes were flashing so much hatred, I thought they were brown too. Thin, she wore jeans and a tight blue shirt and heels that gave her at least three inches on her normal height.

The other one, Serena, had lighter brown hair that fell to below her shoulders in soft waves that reminded me of what mermaids looked like. Dressed in jean shorts and a white t-shirt that both showed off her tan and toned body, she stood barefoot next to her father and stared at me with big brown eyes that didn't have hatred but something else in them.

Disappointment?

As Janelle returned to complaining about my

very existence, I heard Serena say in a pained voice, "You said you knew where she was. You promised you'd find her this time. Where is she?"

I imagined that's what that guy with the pleading eyes would have sounded like if he begged me not to beat the shit out of him. The way she said those words made my chest hurt, and I didn't even know who she was talking about.

But Robert was unmoved by her pleading. Waving off her questions, he said, "Maybe next time, honey. For now, I want you two to welcome Ryder to our home."

He put his arms around both of them, but Janelle slipped out of his hold and stormed off without another word. I didn't have to guess how she felt about me. Serena said nothing more about what was obviously so important to her and simply looked at me with that pleading in her eyes that hadn't worked on her father.

With a nudge from him, she finally said, "Welcome to our home. I hope you like it here."

And with that, she quietly left without another word to her father about whoever she wanted him to find.

Robert walked behind his desk and sat down in his chair as I watched her walk away, her sagging shoulders signaling how defeated she felt. Clearly, it didn't affect her father at all.

"They'll get used to you. Janelle is a little temperamental, but I guess that's to be expected from a girl, even one her age. She's a lot like me, though, so at least she has that going for her. Serena is the polar opposite. She's like her mother. Don't worry about her. She'll take to you like every stray she brings home."

Not that I didn't know I looked like some stray dog compared to them, but the way he said it brought the reality home for sure. In a hurry to get out of there and to wherever he kept the strays he brought home, I said, "Well, if you can just point me in the direction of where you want me to go, I'll get out of your hair."

He shook his head as that crocodile smile spread across his face again. "Not yet. First, I want you to know what I expect of you. So sit down and relax."

Dropping my duffel bag, I sat down in a chair in front of his desk as he'd ordered and listened to hear just what this whole arrangement would involve.

He steepled his fingers in front of him and began. "You'll continue to fight as you did tonight. As I said before, I expect you to continue to win. When you do, you'll get paid, despite the fact that you won't need money as long as you live here."

"I won't need money?" I asked, confused what kind of world this guy lived in that didn't require cash.

Lifting his chin, he shook his head. "No, you won't. Your room and board, along with all the food you want and clothes you need, will be provided. I have a state of the art workout center you're to use to make sure you're in the best shape possible. So you see, you won't need money."

I didn't know if I should question this whole situation that sounded too good to be true, but I asked, "And if I don't win a fight?"

His face grew dark. "Let's cross that bridge when we come to it. For now, I have very few rules, other than you performing in fights like I've seen. No drugs and no romantic attachments. I don't care who you fuck, but don't get involved. I remember being your age, so I don't expect you to live like a monk, but no relationships."

I wasn't a fan of having so much of my life dictated, but assuming I got a room even as big as a broom closet on his estate, maybe it wouldn't be too much of a tradeoff. I wasn't exactly looking for a relationship anyway and I didn't do drugs. Hoping he wasn't about to announce that I had to double as a stable boy or something like that, I smiled.

"Okay. I can live with those."

"And you aren't to tell anyone here what you do. Is that clear?"

"Sure. But if I'm not here as a fighter, what am I supposed to say if someone asks?"

"They won't," he said with a confidence I guessed came from being the boss.

"Got it."

"Good. I'll have my housekeeper take you to your room. For now, you'll have the spare bedroom on this floor."

A short, dark haired woman he called Josephine appeared a few seconds later, so I stood from my chair and grabbed my duffel bag to go with her. I felt like there were a lot more questions I should ask Robert, but he didn't seem interested in talking anymore and picked up the phone to call someone, so I smiled again and moved to leave.

Just before I reached the door, he said, "Oh, Ryder, one more thing."

There it was. The one thing that would make this whole situation unbearable. I slowly turned around and waited for the other shoe to drop.

"Don't even think of doing anything with either of the girls. In that respect, I do care who you fuck."

I thought back to how much Janelle hated me already and easily put the idea of fucking her out of my mind. And Serena? I wasn't sure if she was even legal, and I didn't need that dogging me. An angry father was one thing, but prison was an entirely different story.

She was beautiful, though. There was something about her I could definitely like, if things were different. But no matter how beautiful she was, I wasn't touching that.

"No problem," I answered with confidence, hoping that was the worst thing about living at Erickson's house.

If it was, this would be the best thing to ever happen to me, even if it meant I had to keep fighting. Maybe freedom wasn't all it was cracked up to be anyway.

LOOK FOR THE CORRUPTED LOVE TRILOGY TODAY!
AVAILABLE AT ALL MAJOR RETAILERS

About the Author

K.M. Scott writes contemporary romance stories of sexy, intense, and unforgettable love. A New York Times and USA Today bestselling author, she's been in love with romance since reading her first romance novel in junior high (she was a very curious girl!). Under her Gabrielle Bisset name, she writes erotic paranormal and historical romance. She lives in Pennsylvania with a herd of animals and when she's not writing can be found reading or feeding her TV addiction.

Be sure to visit K.M.'s Facebook page at **facebook.com/kmscottauthor** for all the latest on her books, along with giveaways and other goodies! And to hear all the news on K.M. Scott books first, sign up for her newsletter today and be sure to visit her website at **www. kmscottbooks.com**.

Books by K.M. Scott:

If I Dream (Corrupted Love #1)
If You Fight (Corrupted Love #2)
If We Fall (Corrupted Love #3)

Crash Into Me (Heart of Stone #1)
Fall Into Me (Heart of Stone #2)
Give In To Me (Heart of Stone #3)
Heart of Stone Volume One Box Set
Ever After (Heart of Stone #4)
A Heart of Stone Christmas (Heart of Stone #5)
Unforgettable (Heart of Stone #6)
Unbreakable (Heart of Stone #7)
Heart of Stone Volume Two Box Set

Temptation (Club X #1)
Surrender (Club X #2)
Possession (Club X #3)
Satisfaction (Club X #4)
Acceptance (Club X #5)
The Complete Club X Series Box Set

Crave (Addicted To You #1)
Adore (Addicted To You #2)
Shatter (Addicted To You #3)
Claim (Addicted To You #4)

K.M.'S BOOKS ARE IN AUDIOBOOK TOO!

Books by Gabrielle Bisset:

Vampire Dreams Revamped (A Sons of Navarus Prequel)
Blood Avenged (Sons of Navarus #1)
Blood Betrayed (Sons of Navarus #2)
Longing (A Sons of Navarus Short Story)
Blood Spirit (Sons of Navarus #3)
The Deepest Cut (A Sons of Navarus Short Story)
Blood Prophecy (Sons of Navarus #4)
Blood Craving (Sons of Navarus #5)
Blood Eclipse (Sons of Navarus #6)
The Sons of Navarus Box Set #1
The Sons of Navarus Box Set #2

Stolen Destiny (Destined Ones Duology #1)
Destiny Redeemed (Destined Ones Duology #2)

Love's Master
Masquerade
The Victorian Erotic Romance Trilogy

www.ingramcontent.com/pod-product-compliance
Lightning Source LLC
Chambersburg PA
CBHW032032180726
48284CB00008B/2553